PSYCHIC CHARM

Kate Allenton

This book is a work of fiction. Names, character, places, and incidents are the products of the author's imagination or use fictitiously. Any resemblance to actual events, locals or persons, living or dead, is entirely coincidental.

Published by Coastal Escape Publishing

Discover other titles by Kate Allenton

At http://www.kateallenton.com

ISBN-10:
1-944237-35-6
ISBN-13:
978-1-944237-35-6

DEDICATION

This book is dedicated to my sister, Vicki, because sometimes parkas are really needed in Florida.

And to

My fabulous cousins.

Natalie, Suzanne, Cindy, and Lorenna, you guys always make our family get-together's so much fun. Grab your sunblock and let the husbands watch the kids. This beach read is for each of you. #NewSmyrna2016 or bust.

ACKNOWLEDGMENTS

This book would not be in existence without the love and support of my family and friends who gave me the gentle nudge needed to see this through. Thank you. I appreciate each and every one of you

Chapter 1

Harper gazed out her office window, the warmth of the sun heating her face. The trees below swayed in a late afternoon breeze. If she closed her eyes, she could almost imagine the smell of the salty air as it drifted from the ocean.

The headset pressed against her ear hummed as the caller spoke. She'd know the caller's voice anywhere: silky, sexy, and dangerous. It vibrated, the voice of the kind of man her momma warned her about, and one her Aunt Betty would have tied up in her bed. She was promiscuous like that. A thrill seeker, just like Harper.

You don't walk away from his kind. You walk backward and pull him by his tie, straight to the bed. It was the reason goose bumps covered her arms, and why she locked her doors at night. For all she knew, the body attached to the voice was short, bald, and would think the big O belonged on the music scale. His voice was probably more than his body could ever deliver. That would be her luck, not that she'd ever invite this guy out for coffee to test her theory. Even she had boundaries, not many, but some.

He hadn't told her exactly what he did, and she'd never asked for fear she'd wind up dead. She was too young to die.

"Harper, are you still there?" His voice oozed sex and wrapped around her body, making her all warm and tingly inside. Whatever his profession, he'd make a killing as a phone sex operator. If she closed her eyes, he could be anyone, anywhere. A stranger on the street, a dark, mysterious man from a bar, her gynecologist. She'd never know until she heard him speak.

The truth was, he was just a man on the phone asking her to tap into the energy of a location.

Harper adjusted the headset and moved away from the window. Her gut churned, and yet she couldn't pinpoint why. "I'm still here. Just trying to tap into the energy and get an idea. Where did you say this business trip was taking place?"

"Mexico."

Mexico? Who takes business meetings in Mexico? Drug lords, America's Top 10 Most Wanted hiding from the law, that's who. Not that it was any of her business. She didn't get paid to have an opinion on how this guy ran his life. He paid her for something entirely different: use of her ability to guide him away from danger and uneasy situations. He'd branded her the intuition he'd been born without.

"Mexico," she whispered to herself and closed her eyes. Her gut clenched tight, and her heart pounded frantically. A feeling of unease skittered down her spine. The location wasn't a place she'd soon be visiting. "It doesn't feel right. If I were you, I'd either move it somewhere else or cancel it altogether."

"How about Los Angeles?" He was quick to ask.

Her shoulders immediately relaxed. Her ass cheeks no longer could crack a nut from its shell. That was the place. She felt it in her gut. "That feels a lot better. Relaxing even. Maybe you should extend your stay after the meeting and have a vacation."

His deep laughter filled the line. "You're cute. How much time do we have left?"

His words put a smile on her lips.

"Ten minutes." She ignored the time on the clock. He'd paid for a fifteen-minute psychic call. That was twenty minutes ago. She just couldn't make herself hang up. He was like a drug. A sexy, addictive, in-need-of-rehab drug, and she needed a fix.

"What are you wearing?"

Typical. She'd give him the same answer as last week. He'd asked so many times the question no longer made her blush. "This isn't 1-800-Talk-Dirty-To-Me. I'm wearing clothes."

"You stay dressed a lot."

"People tend to do that when at work."

"Let's play a game. You tell me what you're wearing, and I'll answer one question honestly. Anything you want to know."

"How do I know you're telling the truth?"

"You're psychic."

Harper pressed her lips together. If her sisters knew she was getting personal with a client, well, they'd probably pat her on the back or give her high-fives. They were good like that.

"Fine. I'm wearing a black pencil skirt, a white silk blouse, and three-inch heels."

She totally lied, trying to make herself a more attractive package. Harper ran her sweaty palms down the boyfriend cut jeans she liked to wear loose in case she splurged at lunch and needed the extra room. Jeans that cut into her stomach ranked right up there with an enema.

She glanced down at the coffee stain smack-dab on the lead singer's nose on her favorite concert tee-shirt. She was hopeless.

"Sophisticated, refined, and I bet wearing the heels makes you the perfect height to kiss."

A shrill of excitement traveled down her spine. *Down, girl.*

"Your turn."

"What's your real first name?" The question flew from her mouth before she could stop it. It was the same question she wondered every time he called. Maybe she wanted to know—she had hoped it was Bob or Leroy—to kill some of the fantasy she had after every conversation. *Oh Leroy, take me. That was about as sexy as granny panties.* She needed his name to be like jumping into a bucket of ice.

"That's the question you were waiting to ask? My name?" His voice turned playful. He almost sounded disappointed that she hadn't asked how many inches lay behind his zipper.

"It's only fair; you know mine. Don't tell me you're a Harold or a Eugene." *Please do.*

"This is confidential?"

"Like attorney-client privilege. Okay, well, maybe not that. How about, like a barista and a customer. What's the name they put on your cup?" She'd bet he ordered his extra hot and black.

"Ryker Cage."

"Of course it is." Her hand flew to cover her mouth, and her eyes bulged. She couldn't believe she'd just blurted that out loud.

A low, throaty, very masculine chuckle reached her ears, making her goosebumps add an extra layer. "My turn. What's your favorite dessert?"

"Anything chocolate," she answered without hesitation. "You?"

"The chocolate left on your lips."

She fanned herself, trying to control the heat flooding her body. Blood rushed to her cheeks, and she bit her lip to keep from moaning. This guy was good. Too good. "Okay, I think your time's up."

"Harper." The way he said her name left her breathless.

"Yeah?"

"My time was up thirty minutes ago. We'll talk again soon. You can count on it, princess."

A dial tone filled her ears, and she let out the breath she'd been holding, yanked the headset from her ears, and tossed it onto her desk. What was it with that man? Every time he called, she felt like she'd run a marathon. A sexy, naked, in-the-mud marathon, but a marathon nonetheless. The first time he'd called, he'd asked to speak to a manager, and he'd been asking for her ever since.

Harper's assistant, Patricia, peeked into the office before walking in with a folder and a package that she so politely laid in the inbox. Harper's eyes narrowed as she regarded the extra work. Her day was getting longer by the minute as a headache attempted to form at her temples. She'd bet Ryker knew a good cure for getting rid of headaches. She shoved the thought aside. The folder, the package. She should be thankful for a distraction.

"Is that time sensitive?"

"Would I have brought it in if it wasn't?" Patricia smiled and parked her butt in one of the office chairs. It was her not-so-subtle way to hurry Harper along.

Picking up the folder, Harper flipped it open. The small print on the contract made her eyes cross. "Give me Cliff Notes."

"It's a contract for the new security and IT guy that you finally got your sisters to agree to. He's rewiring the entire building with new stuff for better performance and security."

"Who picked this guy?"

"Quinn, I believe."

Harper flipped to the money amount and what was involved. "Anything in the contract out of the ordinary? Any clauses that agree to the equivalent of kicking a puppy?"

Patricia smiled. "No. I read it. It's a standard contract. One-year term with the cost of monitoring and system upgrades. Nothing strange."

"Will he need to bring the call center down?"

"Afraid so." She pressed her lips together and cringed as if waiting for her bark.

Harper hated to take the company offline. It had been the main reason her sisters always opposed the upgrade, but it really needed to be done. They had a ton of confidential files rotting in the basement that needed to be uploaded into something secure. "Do we really need to take down the entire system?"

"The death threats from the crazies and religious fanatics that want to burn down the building have doubled. I think it's a smart move to get it all done at once."

Harper nodded and scribbled her signature at the bottom before handing it back.

"Coordinate a shutdown for the week before Christmas; then send out an email to the staff and post an announcement on our website for our clients."

Patricia's fingers flew over the keyboard on her phone as if she'd been expecting Harper's request. She'd probably seen it coming. She was gifted too.

"What's in the package?"

She shrugged. "Not sure. A courier dropped it off about fifteen minutes ago. There's no return address, just your name."

Harper lifted the package to her ear and closed her eyes. No ticking. "Thanks."

Patricia rose and headed for the door.

"Hey, Patricia. Is Grace still in the office?"

Patricia turned, walking backward.

"No, Grace was meeting your mother and your Aunt Betty."

Better Grace than Harper. Their mom was a handful all by herself. Throw crazy Aunt Betty, who owned the Thin Blue Line police bar, into the mix, and there was no telling what Grace was having to deal with, or how much she would have to spend on bail.

Harper nodded and returned her attention to the brown package in the non-descript wrapping. Her name was scribbled on the top in a masculine handwriting. She closed her eyes and sensed the package. It was the same energy that cocooned her when she spoke to Ryker, all consuming. Interesting.

She ripped into the brown packing and tossed it into her garbage. A blue box sat inside. It was the kind that women fantasize about from a store where everything is overpriced and shiny.

A card was attached to the delicate white bow.

Harper sat back in the chair and stared at it as if it was a new species yet to be discovered. *He's lost his ever-lovin' mind.*

She could read the card and make sure. Yeah, she could at least read the card.

She ran her finger under the flap and slid the card out.

I have your direct line. I thought it was time that you had mine.

~R

Ryker. His name popped instantly into her mind. How had he known she would ask his name, even if he'd planned to play the game? Maybe he hadn't.

Screw it. Harper eased the lid on the box open, gently pulled back the white tissue paper, and grinned. A can of mace sat next to a phone identical to the one nestled inside her purse. The screen was turned on. The screen saver had the word "Princess."

She picked it out of the box and pressed a button to make the phone come to life. A notification said there was an unread text message. She should have put the phone back. She should have walked away. She should have done a million things. What she shouldn't have done was actually open the message to see what it said.

Princess,
It's time we meet.
Ryker

"Oh, I don't think so, buddy." Who does that?

The phone in her hands rang, making her jump. The caller ID read Ryker. Her finger hovered over the decline button. At the last minute, she answered the call and pressed the phone to her ear.

"This is borderline stalking," she blurted out before he could speak.

"I knew you'd be cautious, but I also know you're curious, so I'll make this easy for you. Regardless if you agree to meet me or not, I've programmed my number into this phone. If you ever need me, just call or text."

"Why would I—"

"If you'd like to meet, LeRochelle at seven. It's public and has security. You can bring the mace. Nothing will happen to you there. Not that I'd ever do anything to harm you."

"You're crazy." And so was she for even considering it. She should have hung up and tossed the phone, but there was something about Ryker that made her keep listening.

"I've been called worse."

"Didn't your momma ever warn you about stranger danger? I could be some deranged psycho chick and you....well, you could be my boring accountant. I'd hate to have to stab your eyes with the toothpick from a fruity drink."

His chuckle filled the line and eased her tension. He had a unique sense of stifling her unease and, what was odd, calming people. That was one of her specialties. "I'm not worried."

"Ryker. How about we keep things professional, and I forget you ever sent this...phone."

"You could, or you could finally, at least, have a face to put with my voice. One drink. If I'm inappropriate, you get up and leave. If I scare you, spray me with mace, and then get up and leave. If I turn out to be the accountant, poke my eyes out, and then leave. I won't even put up a fight."

Harper chewed her bottom lip and clenched her eyes closed as she searched for the energy in his words and the location. Nothing. She was nuts for even considering it.

"My momma is gonna be mad if you make me a statistic. I can see it now. My story will be used in an updated training video on what *not* to do when taking calls." She clutched the phone tighter in her hand. "If I'm going to do this, then I pick the place."

"Where did you have in mind?"

"The Thin Blue Line beach bar." An off-the-wall outlandish location, but a scream in that bar would cut the cop response time to mere seconds, killing the need to write out her obituary before having to leave work. No way was she leaving that job up to her sisters. They'd paint her as a boring spinster cat lady. She was allergic to cats. No obit for her, not with cops within arm's reach. Did they carry guns into bars? She was about to find out.

"The cop hang-out?"

"Take it or leave it, Ryker Cage."

"You're a smart woman taking precautions. I'll meet you on the back deck at seven."

"You got a thing against a crowd of cops?"

"Let's just say, in my line of work, I stay off the radar."

What the hell did he do? A hit man? A mobster? Did Florida even have a mob? Oh God, was he in a gang? And why was he even in town? Warning bells triggered in her mind. Why would she even think this was a good idea?

"Wait, Ryker, I..." The line disconnected and the phone went blank. She shrugged and tossed the phone into her purse, along with the note and the pepper spray.

"Smart, Harper," she chided herself. "I wasn't only getting personal information from a client over the phone, in two hours, I'd know his face." She should be kicking her ass when, in reality, she was already three steps ahead, running a mental inventory of her closet in her head. What did one wear when meeting Mr.-Sexy-Voice-Potential-Killer-Mob-Boss? Shoes for a quick exit or shoes to impress?

Harper picked up her phone and dialed Patricia's extension. "I need coffee, and lots of it."

"Sure."

Harper hung the phone up. She had some digging to do. If she was even thinking about meeting up with the stranger, she'd know everything about him before she left. Twisting her hair up into a bun, she slid her pen through the strands to hold it in place and devoted the next three hours into decoding exactly who was Ryker Cage.

Chapter 2

Ryker glanced at his watch and grinned as he booted up the computer. His fingers flew across the keyboard as he entered the encryption into the secure access site. She was smart not to trust him. He sat back and laced his fingers behind his head, watching Harper do one search after the next on the internet. She'd find only what he wanted her to see. Their mainframe had been an easy mark for an online predator. It *had* been. It wasn't anymore. He'd fixed that little bug. He owed her that much and more.

He sat forward when a website he hadn't been expecting popped up. He hovered his fingers over the keyboard, ready to kill whatever dirt he'd missed. If she knew his real interest in her, she'd be calling him much worse. The guilt still bothered him from his deceit, but having her close enough to watch was worth the betrayal.

She'd lied about her outfit. Her jeans had hung loosely on her hips, her concert tee stretched tight across her breasts, and she'd been wearing flip-flops into work. He knew; he'd been watching. Someone had to.

A knock sounded on the hotel door. A female voice called from the hall. "Room Service."

"Just a minute," he hollered back. Stepping away from the computer for even one second could cost him. He gritted his teeth and squeezed the back of his neck. He'd forgotten he had ordered dinner.

Ryker got up from the laptop, grabbed his gun, and headed for the door. He peered out of the peephole to find a woman, dressed in a standard hotel uniform, standing behind a food cart. Some of the tension in his shoulders eased. No one even knew he was in town, at least no one who mattered.

Ryker shoved the gun into his waistband and lowered his shirt to cover it up. He flicked the lock and pulled the door open.

A petite woman with long, black hair and a forced smile greeted him. She wasn't one of the employees he'd ever seen before.

The name on her badge read Camille. Ryker's brows dipped, and he frowned. Uncertainty clouded him, and an unshakable unease skirting his spine had him reaching behind his back, resting his hand on the butt of the gun.

As if sensing his unease, Camille smiled and lifted the lid to show him the plate. Steam rose from the hot food just as his stomach grumbled. He was acting paranoid. No one knew he was at this hotel. He hadn't even used one of his normal IDs to check in. He used a special one just for this assignment.

"Let me get you a tip." He released the grip on his gun and headed for his wallet sitting next to the computer. Harper had found one of his strategically placed articles. That would ease her worry some.

Ryker saw the woman's reflection on the screen as she moved silently behind him. A knife clutched in her hand and raised ready to strike. He spun just in time to miss her deadly blow. Grabbing her wrist, he wrestled to get the knife away, squeezing her wrist until he heard the crunch of bones and the squeal of agony from her lips. The knife dropped to the floor, and the woman scurried out of his reach and back toward the food cart.

"Who sent you? Who knows I'm here?"

Her lips twisted into a smile as she grabbed another knife.

Ryker's jaw twitched and his nostrils flared as he slipped the gun out of his waistband and squeezed off a shot into her kneecap. The silencer muffled the sound. She screamed and fell to the floor as blood oozed from the wound and onto the floor. He could shoot her in the head. Ryker tilted his head, studying the woman.

"I don't make a habit of fighting women. Tell me who sent you and I'll kill you quickly. Trust me, you don't want me to go slow."

"If I don't kill you, he will. He's made it his mission to destroy every one of you." She used her left hand to throw another knife at him, and Ryker ducked at her feeble attempt. She inched backward toward the door, and he advanced on her, slamming his boot down into the gunshot wound in her leg. Her cry filled the room, and the fight in her diminished as she crumpled.

The alert on his computer dinged. He jerked his head around. A copy of *his* death certificate filled the screen. "Shit."

Ryker whipped his gaze back to the woman who might have just cost him a date. "Now look what you've done."

****

Ryker took a swig of the ice-cold beer. The sound of the waves breaking on the beach behind the deck was his only companion while he stared down at the phone screen. To any onlookers, he looked bored. Which was the opposite of the truth. Harper was still sitting in her car talking to herself. How did he know? He'd breached the bar's security. Not only for himself, but to watch out for her. There might be cops in the bar, but men were men, and when it came to Harper, he refused to take chances. He sadistically enjoyed her struggle to capture her composure and regain her iron will. No way would she drive away. Not his Harper.

She opened the door and then shut it again, twice. She held both phones in her hands before tossing one into her little clutch. Probably the same place she carried the mace. She opened the door once again, and Ryker took another sip. His mouth twitched with amusement around the bottle. This time, she'd gotten out.

"Baby steps, princess."

His pulse quickened as he rubbed the stubble on his jaw. She was dressed exactly as he'd expected; jeans and a T-shirt stretched across her chest, and she'd changed into a pair of tennis shoes for a quick escape. Ryker followed her progression until she was safely inside the bar. The deck was nearly empty. A couple sat in the corner, making out as if nothing in the world mattered. He couldn't remember the last time he'd been comfortable enough to drop his guard.

He hit a few buttons on his phone to hide the surveillance program and took another sip of his beer while silently watching the men in the bar. They'd turned to look at her as she entered. She'd grabbed more than one man's attention, and a few women sneered. Wait until they figure out that Harper was the reason he'd ignored a half dozen women that tried to flirt with him for the last hour. She wasn't making friends tonight.

Her gaze swept across the room, never really stopping on any one person as she made her way to the bar. Ex-FBI Agent Cooper Cruz greeted his sister-in-law with a friendly smile. Ryker had made it a priority to dig into everyone she interacted with, including her family.

Harper ordered a drink and whispered something to Cruz. Her words made him scowl. While she waited for her beer, she closed her eyes. If it was anyone but her, he'd have warned her about leaving herself vulnerable. Within seconds her eyes shot open and landed smack-dab on Ryker's gaze.

I bet she kicked ass at hide and seek.

****

Harper sucked her bottom lip between her teeth and picked up her beer. Butterflies danced in her belly as her mind warred about the brainless move she was about to make. She'd closed her eyes and felt his energy caressing her, as if she could feel his actual touch. She'd known exactly where he was sitting. She pegged him with her gaze as she stepped out onto the deck and sauntered right to his table. The smile in his eyes ignited a sensuous flame, heating her cheeks. Ryker Cage would be the porn star of her wet dreams tonight. Muscles coiled and bunched beneath his black T-shirt. A tattoo peeked out on his arm from beneath his shirt sleeve. Inked and sexy, shit, shit, shit. So much for getting him out of her system. Harper moistened her lips.

"Was I everything you imagined, princess?"

His deep, sensual voice sent a ripple of excitement through her body. Damn.

"Would you mind standing?" she asked as she put her purse on the tall wooden tabletop.

"Sure." He slid off the stool. His long legs were like sturdy trunks. The jeans hung loosely at his tapered waist. His black boots were huge. Double damn, if foot size suggested the length behind his zipper, she'd be walking funny for days, if she ever gave in. He was easily six feet tall, a big-shoe-wearing, pin-her-to-the-wall-ravish-her-body kind of man.

Harper slowly walked around him and clutched her hands into fists, digging her nails into her skin to help keep her grounded. She wasn't ready to scream 'take me' to a damn stranger until she was positive he wasn't armed. Her mom would be mortified, but Aunty Betty would be proud.

She lifted his arms out to his sides. She'd planned to pat him down, mimicking the way they do in the cop shows. It probably didn't matter. He looked like he could snap her like a twig. "I'll make this fast."

"I'd rather you go slow." He turned to face her and took her hands in his warm hold and placed them on his chest.

"When looking for a weapon or accounting ledgers, you need to be thorough."

Muscles bunched beneath her palms as he moved them around his chest and down to his waist. The intensity in his blue eyes made heat pool between her thighs. Her heart jolted and her pulse quickened as she fought the pull of his masculinity. The sight of his shirt stretched tight across his broad chest, and the scent of masculine cologne, was nearly her undoing.

"Always check the waistband." He pulled her body flush against his hard chest, and he moved both of their hands around his body to the back.

"I'd planned to do that without your help." Her voice sounded wanton and not at all strong, as she'd intended. Damn him.

"My apologies." Ryker released his hold and raised his hands to his sides. "I just thought you might enjoy a tour."

"Keep it in your pants, Romeo. Neither one of us is getting naked tonight." She smiled up at him and moved her hands to his sides and then down. She dropped to a crouch and squeezed her hands down the outer part of his legs.

She slowly slid her hands up the inner seam, pausing to look up at him when she felt the tip of his length. Her mouth parted, and she swallowed the pooling saliva before quickly rising back to her feet. Yep, the old wive's tale was true. Shoe size was a pretty accurate comparison, and this guy hung to the right.

"You could have gone higher. I wouldn't have stopped you." He chuckled as she moved away and took her seat. Ryker was a bad, bad boy, and damn if she hadn't been tempted to climb him like a mountain and plant her flag. *Cool yourself, you little hussy.*

"Coop would kick me out for molesting the customers."

Ryker's smile grew. "I doubt that. Are you satisfied I'm not carrying?"

"Sorry. I don't know you."

"Sure you do," he said, retaking his seat. "We've been talking for over a year."

Ryker rested his ankle over one his legs and moved the hem of his jeans out of the way. He pulled a small sheathed blade from his boot and slid it across the table to her. "Never forget to check a man's boots. Keep it. You can gouge out my eyes if you feel threatened."

Humor lurked in the depths of his gaze as she took his knife and covered it with her sweaty palms.

"Are you telling me you're an accountant?"

Ryker chuckled. The sound was a melody to her ears. "No. I'm not an accountant."

"Yeah, that might be a problem." She pulled out a slip of paper from her purse, unfolded it, and slid it across the wood. "Seeing how you're dead. The IRS would probably reject your claims. Maybe I should call the police and tell them that you've made a miraculous recovery."

"If you were going to do that, you wouldn't be here."

"But I could."

He gave her a nod of acknowledgment before taking another long pull from his beer. His face was unreadable. His energy was not. There was only a slight tension in his energy. Her beer sat untouched. No way was she getting drunk around this guy if she was keeping her panties and her wits. She could see he'd take both.

Ryker wasn't like normal men with a wandering gaze. He gave her the entire force of his attention, like a missile seeking its target. If she was smart, she'd walk away and ignore his calls, yet something kept her pinned to the chair.

"I suppose you could. You and I are alike in a lot of ways."

Hardly. Harper wasn't some badass, no matter how many cop shows she'd watched. The only self-defense she knew was thanks to the free class that Coop had given, and even then, she'd been guilt tripped into going.

"How do you figure? I'm a medium with special gifts, and you're...what is it that you do exactly? Oh, wait, let me guess. You dance in a hot male revue? It would explain why you're always calling me about travel."

His smile was flirtatious, hinting at secrets he hadn't yet shared. "Is this a game of twenty questions? I'm willing to play if you are."

"Sure. I'll play. What's your profession?" *Please don't say mob boss. Please don't say mob boss.*

"I don't have a title, but if I had to pick one that was close, I'd say… treasure hunter."

Huh. She hadn't been expecting that. Treasure hunter, a buff Indiana Jones. Yeah, she could see that.

"My turn. When was the last time you had a proper kiss?"

"On my twenty-first birthday. Johnny Parker." She answered a bit too fast. "Do you ever find treasures?"

"All the time."

"Why me?"

He tsked. "You skipped my turn."

She conceded and raised her brow. She had skipped his turn, and he hadn't been drunk enough to notice. Points for him.

"I'm going to kiss you."

"That's not a question. That's a statement."

"Why did you come to the bar?"

"Curiosity. Stupidity." She shrugged. The thought of finally having a face to put with the voice. Although she wouldn't admit it. "Why do you call me?"

"You're my good luck charm."

"I doubt that." Harper finally took a sip of her beer. The cool liquid slid down her throat. She was in a safe place. Her brother-in-law was behind the bar and had promised to keep an eye on her.

Harper set the beer down and studied his beautiful blue eyes. “Why did you fake your death?”

“Why does anyone?”

Her brows dipped as she laced her fingers. “You can’t answer my question with a question. That’s not the way the game is played. You’re running from something. Hiding?” she asked with an unsure shake of her head.

“I’m not sure you’d believe me if I told you the truth.” He took a long pull from his beer.

“Try me.” Did she really want to know? Her momma might be mad that she’d walked into being an accomplice.

“I died so you could live.” His words rang true, free of deception. There was no tension surrounding him.

“I’m pretty sure I’d remember being in need of a life-saving transplant.”

His lips twisted at the corners, sending the butterflies in her belly into a tailspin. “Let’s hope you never do.”

“What does that even mean?”

“You skipped my turn,” he said, rising from his seat.

She saluted her beer in acknowledgment.

“Your sisters and you are special.”

"Is that a question? We can't help that we ride the short bus. It's my mother's fault, or maybe it was the gardener's. I heard he preferred a well-manicured bush." Harper wiggled her brows.

"Your father's in oil and part business owner. Your aunt and brother-in-law are retired FBI."

"You're forgetting the kilt-wearing Highlander. We're all crazy," she said, wiggling her fingers to scare him; instead, she looked like a cheerleader using jazz hands. "How do you know so much about me?"

"It's my job." He rounded the table, crowding her personal space. Her fingers tightened around the knife, and her breath quickened as she fought the urge to pull him closer.

"What's your job?"

"You."

"You're not like a hitman, sent to bump me off? Because I have to tell you I'm a black belt, and my hands are registered as lethal."

He chuckled. "No, you're not."

"Maybe not. But I've got the lungs of a newborn baby. Care to test my theory?"

"I believe you. Have dinner with me tomorrow."

She tsked. "No can do, stranger. I've got plans." And she did. If she didn't show up to her parents' annual Christmas party, her homicide would be the next one the police would be trying to solve.

He cupped her cheek, and she leaned into the warmth of his palm. Her traitorous eyes automatically closed. His words were hot against her ear. “Maybe another time. Sleep well, Harper.”

Harper opened in time to watch him leave via the stairs to the beach. “Sleep well?” she grumbled under her breath. “Not even a kiss?”

It was probably for the best. God forbid he kissed as hot as he looked. She’d never get a restful night’s sleep again.

She rolled her eyes and picked up her drink. When she slept, the least he could do was star in her dreams, every bulging muscle and sensuous whisper.

Chapter 3

Harper adjusted the strap of her bathing suit and tank top before walking into her mother's house. Only in Florida, a week before Christmas, would they have record high temperatures. Her flip-flops smacked the tile as she placed the presents in front of the tree.

"You made it," Quinn said as she approached, placing a flowered lei around Harper's neck.

"Who's bright idea was a full day of celebration. First the luau, and later tonight, black tie. They must have spiked our drinks to make us agree to this."

"I see you're still a smartass." Quinn

winked. “You make me so proud.”

“Did you think I’d change during the six months you were in Scotland?”

“Absolutely not. It’s encoded in your DNA.” She grinned and laced her arm through Harper’s. “Which bikini are you wearing? Please don’t tell me the one with the red polka dots?”

“I burned that thing when I was fourteen, about the same time you were burning your bras and caught the kitchen on fire.”

“I miss those days,” Quinn said, leading Harper out to the back patio. A band was on the stage playing island music, complete with steel drums. The musicians were wearing matching Hawaiian shirts. A line of women dressed in grass skirts and bras made from shells were swinging their hips. “We’re taking bets on which dancer gets so drunk she loses her shells first. You know dad’s friends are horny bastards.”

Harper chuckled. “I’ve got twenty on the blonde in need of a root job. Where did Mom find the entertainment?”

“From me.” Quinn smiled. “If we have to socialize with all these people, we might as well enjoy ourselves.”

There were about fifty people hanging around and in the pool. The chefs were manning the grills, and was that a pig roasting near her mother’s prized roses? A smile formed on Harper's lips. Her mother had to be somewhere in the house hyperventilating.

"There's more people than I thought."

"Well, we Thatcher's do know how to throw a fabulous party."

"You put free booze on the invite, didn't you?"

"Of course." She smiled brightly. "The only way to survive a full day with dad's co-workers and all these strangers is to remember it in a haze."

"Sucks to be you." Harper rubbed Quinn's pregnant belly. "Where's the bar."

Quinn turned toward the wrap-around veranda and pointed toward the house. "Over there. Coop and Aunt Betty elbowed the bartender out of the way and took over. I bet we'll find the young guy hogtied in the pantry with duct tape over his mouth."

"I'd bet money that Aunt Betty has him tied to a bed."

Harper started for the bar, where she'd be perched for most of the party. Ian and Collin were wearing their kilts.

"Nice legs," Harper said as she approached.

"Looking fine, Harper," Ian said with a wink.

"What's your pleasure?" Coop asked, tossing a rag over his shoulder.

"A man that will clean my house."

"We're fresh out of those. Do you want the same as last night?"

"Ohh. You went to the bar on a work day?" Grace said, sliding up to the bar. "What was the occasion?"

"She was meeting a guy," Coop announced, making all the sisters turn in her direction. "She frisked him and everything."

"Ohh, foreplay." Grace's eyes sparkled, and she glanced back at the pool. "Where are you hiding the new play toy?"

"Men and women can be just friends, Grace. It's a fact." Becca said.

"Not in this family." Grace grinned.

"I hardly know the man. No way in hell would I bring him here." Harper narrowed her eyes at Coop. "You suck at keeping secrets." She ignored the heat in her cheeks and leaned over the counter to grab a beer from the ice.

"Sorry, doll. Nothing is off-limits in this family. Isn't that right, babe?" Coop glanced over at Cara sitting in the shade beneath an umbrella, drinking a tall glass of what looked like iced tea.

Cara rubbed her belly as if that should answer the question, and it did. Harper might have had a hand in helping set Cara and Coop up only five months ago, on a case, just so they'd spend time together, but Harper would never admit to it. However, sending the ghost to Coop's house to scare him silly had been all her idea of extra fun. It was the sisterly thing to do.

Quinn popped the top on Harper's beer and dragged her to the umbrella table where Cara was sitting. "So tell us more about your mystery man. Did you do a background check or let Cara touch any of his things to get a read?"

Harper let out a long sigh. "He's a client."

"Nooo." Grace's eyes widened. "You little hussy. You broke company policy."

"You make me so proud." Quinn squeezed Harper like a pleased mother. "I bet he's hot," Quinn said, taking a seat. "I'm right, aren't I?"

"Slap your momma, tie me up, and bring out the whips, kind of hot."

"I wasn't aware you liked that," a voice she recognized all too well said from behind her chair.

"Neither was I," her dad added.

Harper jumped up from the chair as her sisters broke out in laughter. "You! What are you doing here?"

Ryker didn't answer. His easy gaze landed on her lips, his easy grin, playful.

Harper snapped her gaze to her father. "Dad, how do you know this man?"

"Yes, Dad, I think we'd all like that answer." Quinn rose and threaded her arm around Harper's on one side as Grace did the same on the other.

Quinn glanced back at Cara. “Don’t be rude, Cara. Why don’t you shake his hand?”

That was code for “get your ass out of that chair and come do your thing.”

“Absolutely,” she said, holding her stomach as she stood. Just one touch and she’d know every one of his dirty, delectable secrets.

“Girls, I wanted to introduce you to Ryker Cage. He just bought out my shares in your company, and he’s your new partner.”

“You what!” they said in unison.

“Now hold on, girls.” Her dad raised his hand. His cool demeanor was cracking. He had to know Harper and her sisters would put up a fight. Their company had always been family owned. “I can explain.”

“I don’t think there’s an explanation possible that would suffice.” Harper crossed her arms over her chest and gestured to Ryker with her chin. “You should have done your homework. He’s dead.”

Her sisters looked at her as if she’d lost her mind.

“What? I found his death certificate in my search,” she said, as if that would make them understand.

“Not anymore.” He gave her a

conspirator's wink, earning her glare.

"He's the man she met at the bar," Coop said, moving to stand behind Cara and wrapping his arms around her belly, as if to protect them both.

"Dear, take this to the library. You're creating a scene," her mother said, whispering to the group.

"I agree," her father announced and gestured for the others to follow.

Harper grabbed Ryker's arm and waited for the others to get out of earshot. She ignored the heat in her face, knowing it showed. She was ready to spit nails and use him as her target. Of all the nerve. She gave him a tight, you-asshole smile.

"I don't know what your game is, or what you're after, but you can bet your ass I'm going to find out, and then I'm going to use your balls to decorate my Christmas tree."

"That sounds unpleasant." He rested his palm on her arm. "Relax."

Quinn turned at the French doors and hollered, "Are you two coming, or do you need to get a room?"

Ryker held out his arm to gesture her forward.

"I'm not giving you my back. You might stab it with another knife from your boot."

He held out his arm. "Fine. We'll go together." She ignored his arm, walked beside him into the house and showed the way to the library.

The rest of the family, except for her mother, was already waiting inside.

Harper kept her arms crossed. Her entire body vibrated with anger. Her emotion, coupled with that of her sisters, filled every inch of the room. They were all pissed. Nothing her father could say would ever make what he'd done okay.

"I know you girls are upset with me."

"That's an understatement," Harper spat.

"It might help if I introduce myself, Mr. Thatcher."

"Yes," her dad said, flustered. His face flushed, contradicting the stony exterior he showed to everyone outside the family.

Ryker moved to the front of the room and cleared his throat. "My name is Ryker Cage. It is true that I was a client, and Harper stumbled on my death certificate, but I can explain. The death certificate was fabricated."

"Obviously," she said, propping her hand on her hip to stop herself from strangling him.

"My previous employment was as an operative in a special division of the government. We didn't report to any of the letter agencies you've heard of. We oversaw, and were in charge of testing and utilizing individuals with your abilities, to help us achieve our goals."

"You were using me?" Harper asked. The realization hit her like a punch in the gut.

"I was testing your accuracy. There is a difference, Harper."

"Deceit has the same sour taste, no matter how pretty the presentation, Mr. Cage," Quinn said as she moved to stand by Harper, along with her other sisters. The invisible battle line was drawn.

"Yes, well." He let out a lengthy sigh. "I uncovered that one of our subjects was getting his information from outside help, including your hotline, and was pretending to be a detective. I tracked the calls to Harper. Someone found out, and the agency thought it would be best if I disappear until they find the subject. He's trying to cover his tracks, and we believe you're his next target," he said, looking directly into her eyes.

"Why do you think she's his next target?" Grace asked.

"He used two sources, and you're the only one still alive."

"I don't believe you," she whispered into the silent room, barely able to find her voice.

"Oh, for the love of God. Cara, you're up," Quinn said, snapping her fingers. She gestured to Cage.

Cara crossed the room without

hesitation and touched Ryker's shoulder. Coop stood by as her abilities started to work.

"What is she doing?" Ryker asked.

"The test subject's name is Richard Grant." She let go of his arm and grabbed Coop's hand. "He's telling the truth." She turned to Harper. "And Mr. Cage has been watching you. He's got surveillance around your home. He's watched you go to work. He even watched you when you were debating to go into the bar."

His gaze was bold and assessing as Cara's words registered. Richard Grant? The name was vaguely familiar, but not enough to remember their conversations. She opened her mouth, and nothing came out. She slowly started to shake her head. "I don't remember a Grant."

"Well, if that's not just creepy." Grace groaned and hit Harper's shoulder. "You've got your own little hot stalker. I want one."

"That's a nifty trick. We should have been watching you, too, it seems," he said to Cara.

"Back off," Coop growled.

Ryker held up his hands. "I'm not the bad guy here. I saw a problem, and I stepped in to stop it."

"And buying into the company? How does that fit into your plans?"

"I needed to be close, even if you guys

protested. Your father agreed, so we came to an arrangement. Either he or you can buy back the shares when Richard Grant is out of the picture. It was a stipulation your father insisted on." Ryker slid his hands into his pocket and licked his lips. "Twenty-two seconds...that's the amount of time it took me to hack your database. Two minutes was the amount of time it took me to break in to set up the surveillance. Thirty is the amount of times Harper has been vulnerable in just the last two days. One...is the number of bullets it will take to kill her. Think of me as her bulletproof vest."

Ice slid down Harper's spine as she bit her tongue. "What do you get out of it for helping me...us?"

"I can answer that," Aunt Betty said, walking into the library. "He needs your help."

"With what?" Harper asked, pegging Ryker with her gaze, unable to let go of his deceit.

"Locating something. I'm not sure what it is yet, but he's actively searching for something."

"I'm going to need a stronger drink," Harper said, spinning on her heels and storming out of the library. Her mind was hazy as she replayed every word he'd ever told her. The flirting, the twenty questions, the calls. She'd been his research. A freakin' pawn. She walked into the kitchen and straight to the liquor cabinet. No way was she going outside and facing all of those nameless people while pasting a smile on her face. No amount of Christmas cheer could fix her mood.

She grabbed a bottle of tequila and set it on the counter. Bracing her hands on the countertop, she lowered her head and squeezed her eyes closed. Of all her clients, why him? Hell, why her?

"I take it that didn't go well, lass?" Ian asked, resting his hip on the counter.

"No." She sighed, lifting her gaze. "It seems we have a new partner, and worse than that, he's been stalking me because he has a hidden agenda."

"I'm no' surprised. When you Thatchers get into trouble, it's always the equivalent of a 747 jumbo jet trying to land in Times Square."

Laughter escaped from Harper's lips. "Those are wise words, MacDougall. You should forget you know us and run back to Scotland."

"Nay, lass. You're my new entertainment." He gave her a lopsided grin as she twisted the top off the bottle.

"What would you do if you were a target, and being manipulated?"

Ian rested his hand on the top of the bottle. "I'd do what my father did before me, and his father before him. I'd draw my sword and fight to the death. I wouldn't wait for the danger to find me. I'd charge all in and take them all by surprise. Do you know what I like about you sisters?"

"We have a pulse and boobs?"

He smiled and winked. "Besides that. You're like female Highlanders. The lot of you are fierce in your own right. You seize the moment to help when you can and deal with the consequence after the fact. Take a look at your sisters. Quinn was told to forget the emerald. Cara was dead set against helping Coop. It only makes sense that you'll handle this with the same finesse and stubbornness. Besides, if that disnae work, then I'll lend you a spare sword and fight by your side until we cut down each and every threat that stands to harm the others or you. You have the MacDougall word."

"You're right," she said, recapping the liquor. "I am a fighter."

"Aye, you come from a long line of them, lass."

Chapter 4

The loud voices and arguing in the library silenced as Harper stomped in, grabbed Ryker's hand, and hauled him out. She didn't stop until she had him inside her old bedroom with the door closed. She leaned back against the wood and blew the hair out of her eyes.

Ryker gave her a lopsided grin. "If you wanted to get me into your bedroom, all you had to do was ask."

"Cut the flirting. When was I vulnerable?"

"Excuse me?"

"When?" she demanded.

"The coffee shop when you spilled your coffee on your concert T-shirt. In the bar parking lot, when you were debating to come inside and meet me, which was stupid by the way. I could have been anybody. I could have done anything." He let out a sigh. "When you were standing, by your window at work, talking on the phone to me. When you opened an unknown package. When your porch light went out and you didn't replace it."

"That was you?"

"Yes. You probably have a short. I've fixed it three times. Would you like me to continue?"

"If I help you find Grant, and whatever else it is you're searching for, you'll leave us alone and let us buy back my father's shares?"

"Is that what you want?"

"Stop answering my questions with another question," she demanded. "This isn't a game. This is my life, my company. So just....stop." She searched his eyes for his answer, and the emotions surrounding him for a clue, and she was smacked in the gut with his desire.

She stopped herself from licking her lips.

"Fine," he said, tilting his head in acknowledgment. "As long as you don't argue with me about helping you, and in return help me find what I'm looking for, I'll sign everything back over. Believe it or not, Harper, I quit testing you months ago.

Every call after that was because I enjoyed our talks."

She stood on her tiptoes, trying to look him in the eye. His lips twitched at her effort, and he lowered his head.

She raised her brow and smiled before pressing her lips to his in a surprise kiss. His lips were soft yet firm, and she fought to ignore the zap of awareness that hit her. The kiss was quick and unnecessary, but she wanted to level the playing field.

"You're not right about everything, Cage. You didn't kiss me; I kissed you. We'll start tonight at the black tie party at the country club. I'll be in public and a sitting target. That and my home are the best places to attack."

"I agree," he said as his brows dipped, and the look of confusion on his face made her grin. "Most women would be scared."

"I'm not scared. I'm worse. I'm pissed." Aggravation clawed at her from his betrayal. Trust hadn't just flown out the window. It had landed hard on the pavement and then been run over by an eighteen-wheeler before being flung into a cage of bulls, stomped and torn to shreds. Trust…there was none.

"What time should I pick you up?" he asked.

"You shouldn't. That defeats the purpose of being an easy target." She stepped around him and left him standing in her room. She had less than eight hours to pull a plan out of her ass that included staying alive, and for that, she was going to need a miracle and a little help from the dead.

****

Harper stood with her sisters on the patio outside the country club. Each looked on, amused at the chaos inside. Beneath the twinkling lights around the room, and the soft beat of the music, swarmed fifteen ghosts that had come to help.

"Who's Redbeard?" Harper asked the others as she scanned the otherworldly floating among the living in the ballroom.

"He's Collin's great-great something. You know those Highlanders are always looking for a fight."

Harper nudged her. "He does realize that sword he's swinging can't actually hurt the living?"

"I'm not sure he cares," Quinn answered.

"And the one who looks bored? Who does he belong to?"

"Oh, you remember him. He's the one that haunted my ass over the emerald," Quinn said turning her back to the ballroom to face her sisters. "It's game time, ladies. Collin, Coop, and Ian have eyes on the doors."

"Where's Ryker?" Harper shouldn't care where he was. It almost pained her to ask. Almost.

Cara shared a grin with Quinn before turning back to Harper. "He's doing surveillance from the van."

"With Aunt Betty," Quinn said before she broke out in laughter.

Harper's smile spread into a full-out grin. He deserved more than a couple hours with the crazy woman. He deserved years. Only then would she feel a little less betrayed. No matter that his excuse had been to save her life.

Grace put her hand into the middle of the circle, and the rest of their sisters did the same. "No one comes into our house and fucks with us. Light the fires and burn the bras. It's time we kicked some motherfucking balls. Pencil dick on three."

They pumped their hands together three times and yelled, "Pencil dick," all together, as if they were a football team about to take the field. The guests closest to the patio doors turned and gasped. Harper grinned and curtseyed.

"Did you just yell pencil dick?" Ryker's smooth, silky voice asked into the receiver in her ear.

"Why? Are you offended?" Harper asked, walking into the ballroom behind her sisters. The lot of them made a sight.

Five women on a manhunt, surrounded by conspirator ghosts helping with surveillance.

"I think you know better. You care to play another round of twenty questions or maybe a different game, like show and tell?"

"Group channel here, guys," Cooper growled. "No one that isn't married is playing hide the salami."

"Hey…" Ian chimed in. "Speak for yourself."

"You don't count, Ian," Collin said and chuckled.

"He's not getting lucky either," Becca said with a grin.

"I second that." Grace said with a chuckle.

The sisters split up around the room, each taking a direction and circling the partygoers as if they were prey. One of them was bound to recognize an unwelcome face or get a funky vibe. Ghosts swirled in and out of groups, stopping to listen to conversations.

"He's not going to know anyone," Harper said, trying to keep her lips as still as possible as she talked, hoping not to look like she belonged in a mental institution for having a conversation with herself. "He won't be in a crowd. Look for loners."

"Or wait staff," Becca said.

Harper hadn't thought about the waiters and waitresses mingling with the guests, offering food and hors d'oeuvres. If someone actually wanted her dead and knew her better, all they'd have to do was put arsenic in the chocolate desserts. She could sniff out dessert fifty yards away, in a room full of sweaty cowboys.

She grabbed a glass of wine from a passing waitress, knowing the person after her was male. Still, it was just for show. No way was she drinking anything unless she personally pulled the cork.

Harper stood in front of the dessert table and inwardly cursed that she wouldn't be sampling any of that sugar tonight.

"Don't even think about it," Quinn said into the earpiece. "We don't know if any of that is contaminated."

"No one else is getting sick," Harper mumbled as a man grabbed a pastry and shoved it into his mouth as he walked by. Her heart dropped into the pit of her empty stomach.

"Not yet," Quinn said. "Give them a few hours, and if no one's croaked, only then can you eat."

"They need a special place in hell to string a man up by his balls for denying me the right to eat perfectly fine chocolate," Harper mumbled and spun around, back to the crowd. Her night was getting longer, and she was getting more pissy by the minute.

Three hours went by, and the party was winding down. The unwrapped gifts they'd collected for the orphanage for Christmas had exceeded previous years. Thank God it wasn't her year to organize the delivery to the orphanage so the orphans had something to open on Christmas Day. Harper plopped down at an empty table and kicked off her shoes to alleviate the pain in her feet. Her stomach grumbled in protest just from looking at the half-eaten cake someone had left behind. The bottled water she drank left her feeling bloated and waterlogged. How was anyone supposed to endure these parties if not in a tipsy haze?

A strong hand landed on her shoulder, making her body tense until she locked eyes with the owner. Ryker Cage.

"I thought you could use this. I know I could." He lifted the unopened bottle of champagne and set two flutes on the table.

"You must be a mind reader."

He smiled without responding, making quick haste of opening the bottle. He poured them each a glass and handed her one. "Looks like Richard didn't like the venue."

Richard Grant. A name she'd now take with her to the grave. The only man able to separate her from her chocolate deserved to die a slow, painful death. A smile slipped on her lips. “I guess we’ll save the ball crushing for another day unless, of course, I find him hiding under my bed.”

Ryker sat back in the chair and held her gaze. There was something deep and mesmerizing in his eyes that shielded his mystery. She’d miss their weekly chats when everything was said and done. Ryker’s gaze caressed her face and dropped to her lips. “I’m sorry I couldn’t come clean early on.”

“Me too.” Those two little words spoke volumes, but that was all he deserved.

Ryker lifted Harper’s foot to his lap. She could feel the bulge in his pants as he settled his big fingers in the ball of her foot. He pressed, making her eyes slide closed in momentary bliss. A soft moan slipped from her lips. He worked the soreness out of one, and then she lifted the other one and wiggled it in his face. He chuckled.

“You’re kind of pushy,” he said through his smile and chuckled.

“You offered.” Harper shrugged and sipped her champagne. Damn him. Not only was he hung like a bull, but he also had magical fingers.

“Is that all it takes because I have a lot more to offer, if you just say the word.”

She slipped her feet free and tucked them back into her shoes. “Office relationships are frowned upon at our company. I guess my dad didn’t give you the rule book.” She tsked and smiled as she rose.

“Good thing this isn’t a relationship.” He rose, crowding her with his body. His warm palm cupped her arm as he lifted her chin to meet his gaze. Harper’s entire body went from half asleep to electrified just by his touch. He leaned in, and she held her breath.

His breath was hot in her ear. He whispered, “Come home with me.”

He pressed a sensuous kiss at the nape of her neck.

“Deep throat that microphone like a rock star.” Quinn’s voice broke Harper from the erotic haze, coming loud and clear over the transmitter still in her ear.

“Don’t be ridiculous. You don’t even know where home is,” Cara said.

“Oh, I don’t know. You should do him and get it out of your system. You might not get another chance. There is a killer that wants you dead, after all,” Grace said.

“She’s got enough on her plate. Don’t give her anymore ideas.” Becca added.

“Spoil sport.” Quinn replied.

Pain pierced Harper’s temple. The running commentary was giving Harper a headache. She lowered her head and pulled the transmitter out of her ear, holding it up for Ryker to see before shoving it in his coat pocket. His lips twisted into a smile.

"What's the consensus?"

"It's a tie. Two for me stripping you down and making you a notch on my bed post, and two for me watching you in the rearview mirror.

Ryker's hands landed on Harper's waist and slid down the silky fabric of her dress to cup her hips. "Which sisters said no?"

His question made her smile. Like she'd ever give him help getting Cara or Becca to agree. "It doesn't matter. If I listened to everything they said, I'd either be in a psychiatric ward or already in my grave. I make my own decisions and"—she shook her head and patted his lapel—"you should have come clean from the beginning. I don't sleep with men I don't trust. I'm going home and going to bed...alone. I have to get up early and go into work."

"I thought you were closed the entire week?" His brows dipped as he studied her.

"We are," she said, not giving him any more information. He might be part owner in the company, but damned if she was going to acknowledge it.

Harper slid around him and waved to

her sisters, who were standing by the bar, before she headed toward the exit. If there was a stalker outside or hiding in her car, he was going to get what he had coming. She was horny, hungry, and sober. It was a deadly combination.

****

"You're just going to let her walk out?" Crazy Aunt Betty said as she approached. Ryker had endured the last three hours with the woman who talked his ear off about sexual positions as she "accidentally" groped him.

"I've got surveillance at her house and a tracker on her car," he said, not worried that Harper wouldn't make it home in one piece. He could view her progress with a few simple clicks on his phone.

"You know my nieces always fight the attraction in the beginning. Take her sister, Cara. We had to make up a dangerous situation just so she'd spend time with Cooper. Quinn...needed to be stranded in another country to help her Highlander. Grace and Becca will be the same. Harper, though....she's got walls a mile tall. Cracking through won't be an easy feat."

Betty's words made him pause. Why would she think his intentions were anything more than sex and keeping

Harper alive? He wasn't a stay-around type guy. He was the type of guy who talked women out of their panties and then never looked back.

"I think you've got the wrong idea," he said. "I'm not the kind of guy you bring home to mom, unless you're trying to piss her off."

Aunt Betty crossed her arms over her chest. "Is that so?"

"Of course," he said in a firm voice, as if he was trying to convince them both. "She's an assignment. You, of all people, should understand that."

"Funny." She grinned. "You've already met her mother and her father, and you were the one to instigate it. You do realize that we can keep her safe, don't you?" Betty winked and walked off.

Her question rankled him, creating a certain void in his chest where his heart should be. It was possible they could keep her safe, but he could do it better. He knew the threat better than most.

Chapter 5

Ryker unlocked the door to his home, which, on the outside, looked like an abandoned warehouse. He used it only in case of emergencies, preferring hotel food over cooking for himself. After the attempted assassination at the hotel, he had no choice. He reset the security alarm before stepping onto the lift up to the top floor to his residence. The nicely furnished apartment had been compliments of Eve, and he didn't have the heart to change a thing. He rubbed his chest to ease his aching heart as he gazed at the floral paintings she'd hung on his walls. He had a whole storage shed full of her others, which used to hang in her studio. He'd been careless back then, but not anymore. He pressed a kiss to his fingers and touched his favorite painting.

"It's almost over. He's going to come after her like he did you, only this time I'll be there to stop him."

He flicked on the power of the six flat screens hanging on the wall and booted his personal computer. He was in for a long night.

Ryker walked into the kitchen. The stainless steel pans hanging above the island shined, confirming that Rosemary was still keeping the place clean. He yanked the fridge open to find it bare, save the six pack of Miller Lite and a couple cans of Dr. Pepper he'd left the last time he'd been back. Grabbing a can of soda, he walked back into the open living room. The room had a dual personality, much like his own. One part looked like command central, with high-tech computers and equipment and the wall full of monitors, the best that money could buy. The other side of the room looked like a normal living space, complete with leather sofas, his favorite La-Z-Boy, and another big screen TV hanging on the wall. The life he used to have.

He opened the soda and took a sip as he slid into his computer chair. The leather creaked beneath his weight as he pulled up the surveillance around

Harper's house on three screens, and on the other three, he pulled up the hidden cameras he'd placed inside her residence. He hit the switch to turn on the audio. He'd keep her safe. He wouldn't make the same mistake again.

Harper had already made it home. She'd changed into yoga pants and a tank top. Her outfit of choice when she was home alone. His outfit of choice when he watched her. The tank top hugged the swells of her breasts. The yoga pants clung to her every mouthwatering curve. He would have definitely seduced her into bed if given the chance. He still might.

He engaged the motion sensors around the perimeter of her house. They'd trigger an alert through his system if anyone got too close. Not that she had many visitors during the week. A few of her sisters and the family friends, including the kilt-wearing Ian MacDougall, had been within an arm's reach of her all night.

Harper booted her laptop and disappeared into her kitchen, returning with a glass of wine. She was one of the easier ones to watch. He watched as she surfed the web, and only then did he start to play. Within seconds, he'd taken remote command of her computer and started a video of a woman thoroughly being kissed on the bed. He typed a message across the screen.

This could be you.

Her eyes narrowed as her gaze shifted around her house. He knew what she was looking for, not that she'd ever find his hiding spots. She picked up her phone, punishingly pressing the keyboard to send him a message.

You have video in my house!?!?!?!?!?!?

Ryker changed the video for her to one of cats and chuckled before he called her.

"What kind of protector would I be if I didn't?"

"You aren't a protector; you're a voyeur." She rose from her couch, walked to the window and peeked outside.

"Calling me a voyeur makes it sound like I'm watching you have sex. I haven't been that lucky."

"And you won't be," she said, returning to her computer. She logged off, put the laptop away and picked up her wine, sloshing it around while gesturing with her hands. "I'm never having sex in these walls again. I'm going to have to move or rent a hotel. Now, look what you've made me do."

He remembered saying those words the day before to the woman who'd tried to filet him. Just one more reminder why he needed to keep his head in the game. His enemies would eat her for lunch and leave her broken, if not dead. "Get some rest, Harper. You look tired."

"Bite me," she said and took a sip of her wine, resettling into her favorite spot on the couch. "How do you even know this Richard guy is coming for me? We haven't seen him yet. He can't be very efficient if he's missed all those thirty times I've been vulnerable. How do I even know you're telling the truth?"

"Because you aren't the only one he used." Ryker's answer tasted like razor blades going down his throat. All he heard was the quick intake of her breath. Her picture on the screen told him so much more. The color had drained from her face. Her glass held frozen in mid-air. She was scared, and she damn well better be.

"Who else?" Her words were whispered.

"My sister-in-law. Get some sleep, Harper. You're safe tonight. You have my word."

With that, he hung up. Saying the words made his heart clench. He watched Harper on the screen. She sat with the phone clutched in her hand and her head down. He couldn't read her expression, but he didn't have to. He could imagine her thoughts. What if it had been one of her sisters who had been killed? That alone would have her being more vigilant.

He remembered the hurt in Eve's eyes when she'd finally told her family about her abilities. The way her entire family shunned her and made her feel like a freak for her gifts, suggesting she join the military like her step-brother. They'd destroyed her spirit. She'd been broken, and he'd been the one to pick up the pieces. It was his fault that she'd ever entertained the idea of working for his company six months prior to her big family reveal. It was she who confided in the Thatcher sisters and asked for directions about her career. Unbeknownst to them, they'd helped him pull her out of the depression even his brother couldn't see.

Ryker's urging her to use her abilities had cost her; she paid with her life. It was his fault she was dead. He'd be damned if he let anyone hurt Harper. He wouldn't let Richard Grant anywhere near her. Not while he was watching.

****

After a sleepless night, Ryker had just stepped out of the shower and now ran a towel over his head as he flipped through the screens in his hunt for Harper. He found her in her room, packing a bag. He tossed the towel over a chair and grabbed his phone, dialing her number. She paused when it rang and then ignored the damn phone. She was going to run. He could feel it in every fiber of his bones.

Ryker hurried to dress, never letting his eyes stray from the computer for more than a few seconds. If he was going to stop her, he needed to get to her and fast. When she picked up the phone, he couldn't see who she was calling, so he clicked on the audio.

"Hey, it's me," she said in a hushed tone, so he turned up the volume. "You remember our little talk? You were right, and I need your help."

He couldn't hear who she was talking to or what was being said. The one-way conversation had him clenching his teeth as he slipped a foot into his boot.

"You're on sister duty. Keep them safe."

What the hell did the woman think she was doing? And where the hell was she headed? She couldn't possibly have a clue on where to find Richard. If she had, she would have said something, wouldn't she?"

Harper slid her suitcase closed, and Ryker had to switch screens to follow as she locked up her house and stepped outside. Her gaze scanned the streets before she got into a fucking cab. Had she known about the GPS on her car?

A flash of the cab company name on the side of the car and a few minutes later, he had hacked into their system and pulled up the cab's GPS. He watched as it took her to the last place he ever thought she'd go. Her office.

He didn't know if he should be relieved or pissed off. Ryker grabbed his keys, and within minutes, he was dodging traffic toward her destination. If he didn't catch her there, he might not be able to track her any further. It was his only hope of stopping whatever game she was playing.

Chapter 6

Harper unlocked the building and was sure to lock the door after her before she set her suitcase behind the security desk and punched the call button on the elevator. The building was dark except for the morning light streaming through the windows. She wasn't used to being the only one in the building, but she wasn't scared. The building held its own energy from everyone who crossed the threshold. She stepped out onto her floor and flicked on a few lights, lighting the way toward her office. She had work to do all right, and it had nothing to do with the new security system that was being installed tomorrow.

She'd boot her computer and do what she did best. There was only one way she was going to find Richard Grant, and that was to retrace every conversation and every call to figure out who the bastard was and what exactly she'd told him. Ian's words came back to her, take the fight to him, and that was exactly what she planned to do. She might not actually be able to take him out, if and when she found him, but she had faith that Ryker wasn't far behind, and he could do all the manual labor.

Harper didn't take many calls anymore. She had only about a dozen or so normal clients that would call her. Finding her mystery man should be a piece of cake.

She pulled up the call logs and the associated recordings, quickly dismissed all of Ryker's, and moved on to remove all of the female callers. That left her with four clients, and out of those four clients, it could have been any one of them. She was about to hit play on the first recording when a shadow caught her eye. Ryker was standing at her door.

"What the hell do you think you're doing?" His usually sexy voice was demanding and gruff. His hair was still wet, his face cleanly shaved. He looked scrumptious. An early morning tryst crossed her mind. No one would be the wiser.

"Working." She smiled up at him. "But you can actually help. When Richard called, and turned over my information to whomever the hell it is you work for, what was the information? That will help me narrow down our conversations."

His brows dipped, and the muscles in his jaw ticked. He was confused, a look she was sure not many people had ever seen.

He pushed off the doorjamb and rounded the desk. His arms crossed over his big muscular chest. *Focus.* She shook her head as her fingers hovered over the keyboard, waiting for his reply.

"They tested him at first."

"Like you tested me?"

"Yeah, only his was different. They gave him a picture of a box and told him he had a day to figure out what was in it. He said that the visions came to him in dreams."

"A box?" she asked, vaguely remembering the conversation. "Pictures of a pineapple and a cat?"

"Yeah." Ryker dropped his arms to his sides as she typed the word pineapple in the search box. Within seconds, she had the audio transcript pulled up. She hit

Play on the audio and listened to the recording.

Ryker rested his hands on the back of her seat as he stood behind her. He smelled of fresh rain with a hint of something she couldn't identify. A smell that she'd come to associate with him.

His fingers dug into her seat and the tension in the air thickened as he listened to the conversation. If he could have crawled through the Internet and straight to that voice, he would have silenced it for good. His energy turned...violent.

"Is that him?" Harper asked, glancing up.

Ryker's jaw clenched as he nodded. She pulled up all of the corresponding audio and call logs made from the same number. She went straight to the last one, which was two months prior and listened.

"Ms. Thatcher, this is Detective Grant. I'm searching for a missing thumb drive that is crucial to a case. Can you help me track its location?"

Harper chewed her bottom lip between her teeth.

"Can you give me the name of the last person to have it?"

"Eve Cage."

Pain tore through Harper's heart and blazed a trail of regret through her body until she thought she might be sick. She lowered her head. She remembered the call verbatim. She hadn't given him a direct location but a city. Harper hit Pause and turned to look at Ryker. His mouth parted slightly as he stared blankly at the screen.

"I'm so sorry," Harper said, rising from her seat. "We vet all law enforcement. He had to have passed our backgrounds in order to get through to me."

"Hit Play."

"Ryker," she pleaded, knowing he probably didn't need to hear the rest. "Please, don't do this."

"Hit Play." He growled his demand.

When she didn't make a move to hit the button, trying to spare him, and herself, from what she knew would come next, he reached around her and jabbed the button himself.

"Give me a minute," she'd said in the recording. She could hear her breaths over the recording as she'd tried to connect. "Carson City."

"And the thumb drive?"

"Behind a tree." Harper had said it more as a question than a statement.

"I can't do this," Ryker said, straightening, unable to look her in the eye. "She's dead because of you."

All fight left her body. Her hands fell to her sides. The knots in her belly twisted into a tight ball of regret as she watched Ryker walk toward the door. "Ryker, wait."

Her words stopped him, yet he didn't turn around. He wouldn't look at her, and she couldn't blame him. No words would ever make things right, but she had to try. "I'm so sorry. I'll track this bastard down, and I'll find him if it's the last thing I do."

"You've done enough." His words were but a whisper, but the impact was a direct hit against her heart, shattering it into a million pieces. He walked out without looking back, without another word. He was just gone.

How could she have been so stupid? She should have asked more questions. She should have felt the caller's energy. There were a billion things she should have done, and none of them included answering the caller's question.

Harper plopped down into her chair as a tear slid down her cheek. Ryker Cage's personal hell was all her fault. She didn't know how long she sat in that same position, hoping that he'd come back in and tell her that she was wrong, but deep down, she knew she'd never hear those words.

Her phone rang, pulling her from the haze of self-pity. She answered it and swallowed around the lump in her throat to find her voice.

"Where is he?" Aunt Betty asked.

"Gone."

Chapter 7

Ryker walked along the beach in a daze, trying to make sense out of what he'd heard—Richard asking Harper for Eve's location and she'd fucking told him. Ryker rubbed at the soreness in his chest. Here he was trying to save the one woman who had contributed to Eve's death. She might not have jabbed the knife, but she was responsible just the same.

Not even the peaceful ocean breeze could cool the heat brimming inside as the phone conversation replayed in his mind. He should have seen this coming. He should have figured out that Richard hadn't found Eve on his own. He'd used a psychic to track down, Eve. Harper had given him the damn city. She might as well have just drawn him a map. The picture of Eve and Ryker lying in shattered glass on her floor should have been his first clue how Richard had figured out their connection.

His sister-in-law had called him the same day she'd died. She'd said she had proof that would expose the organization and their twisted game of using psychics for their own personal gain. She was going to meet him the next day. They were going to go to the press together. Ryker hadn't found the evidence she suggested. No memory drive had ever been found. That was one of the things that Ryker needed Harper to help him with. Damn Eve, and damn Harper.

Thinking of them both, he realized they were a lot alike. Both headstrong, both psychic, and both connected to him.

Ryker turned from his view of the ocean to head back to his car and, only then, realized he was farther down the beach than he thought. The Thin Blue Line bar was on the shore behind him. Betty was leaning against the railing with her fingers laced, watching from above.

He stood his ground as she jogged down the steps off the deck and headed in his direction. The crazy-ass woman probably already knew what had happened. What was left to say?

"You didn't tell her the whole truth,"

she said, coming to a stop in front of him, her arms crossed over her chest. Her spiked hair was no longer pink but now blue in the sunset.

"Yeah well...what are you, a mind reader?" Unsure what this woman knew, he slipped his hands into his pockets and bit his tongue to keep himself from saying something that might have Betty shooting him on the spot.

"I don't need to be," she said, taking his arm and walking up toward the bar. "You know what you need?"

"To find Richard Grant." His answer came fast and quick.

"Yeah, well..." She lifted her brow and walked up onto the back deck.

She led the way into the bar, and he stopped in his tracks.

There were four pairs of female eyes shooting daggers in his direction. The last thing he needed was Harper's damn sisters.

"Sit," Quinn said while gesturing to a chair. Ryker didn't budge, earning Quinn's evil gaze.

"I'd sit if you value your balls," Ian said, walking up behind Ryker. "Quinn doesn't like to be told no. She put me on my knees in two seconds flat when we first met, and I'm bigger than you."

Ryker could see the redhead's temper. It matched her hair. He moved to a table and straddled a chair.

Quinn clasped her hands behind her back and began to pace like a teacher in front of a classroom of children. "When we work with law enforcement, we do a thorough background." She glanced at Ryker. "You'd know that if you looked." She raised a brow and continued talking. "We call references; we call the commanding officers; hell, we verify the credentials prior to the first call." Quinn stopped and crossed her arms over her chest. "Harper found your death certificate, and she wasn't even trying."

He started to rise when hands clamped on both of his shoulders and pushed down. A Highlander on each side. "She's no' done yet, lad."

Cara crossed the room and tossed a file onto the table. "What Quinn hasn't told you is that we keep copious records on everyone we talk to. We not only record their calls for posterity's sake, but we also keep track of everything from credit cards to phone records. Grant had people vouching for him. He isn't the only player in this game."

Becca, the quiet one of the bunch, crossed her arms over her chest. "In that file, you'll find everything we kept, including the audio authorization from the commanding officer. You'll find a transcript of every call and word spoken up until the last syllable."

"I didn't find anything on your server," Ryker grumbled and flipped the file open to the first page. A picture of Richard Grant in a police uniform and his fake employment details were on the front page.

"We don't keep it on our mainframe," Cara said, clasping her hands together. "We're well aware of our lack of security. It's why we're having a new system installed tomorrow."

He scanned the documents. The call log would help him pinpoint Richard's last location, and maybe from there, he'd be able to pick up his trail, but that meant one thing. Harper would be vulnerable. That ache in his chest twisted into a knot.

"Everyone has skeletons, Mr. Cage." Quinn rested her hand on her belly.

True. He had plenty of both.

"Some innocent and some intentional. Did you ever stop to think that Harper is just as much a victim in this mess as was your sister-in-law?"

"Harper genuinely thought she was helping the authorities. She would never put an innocent's life in danger, and if you can't see that about her, then you don't know her at all." Quinn's gaze softened.

****

Harper had spilled her guts to her aunt—what had happened, when it happened, every dirty detail—when Betty had shown up just minutes after Ryker had left. She'd pulled the file and handed it to her without even knowing what proof they'd kept inside. She'd created enough damage to last a lifetime. She wasn't a fighter like Quinn. She wasn't a peacekeeper like Becca. She was something in between. Even if she could find Richard Grant, there was nothing she could do to the man, and nothing she could ever say to make things right with Ryker, but she could try.

She made the last stroke with her pencil before opening her eyes. The image was similar to the one she'd seen when she'd said the proof was in the trees. It wasn't a familiar location. No palm trees, just big pines near a beautiful stream. Even if she couldn't bring his sister back, she could at least help him find what everyone was searching for.

Harper stretched her neck from side to side and turned toward the window to find the sun had already started to set. So much for her big quest to locate and bring down Grant. She'd been gung-ho that morning when she'd come to her senses and acknowledged she didn't know how to fight. Her suitcase was downstairs. Where in the world had she thought this trip down memory lane was taking her? She was such an idiot.

Harper called a cab, flicked the lights off, and headed downstairs to retrieve her bag. She walked outside, pulling her suitcase behind her, and locked the building up nice and tight.

"Harper Thatcher?"

The voice made her jump and spin around, thinking the cab company had been quick. There was no cab on the street, only a man in jeans and a tee shirt staring at her.

"Yes?" she asked, putting her luggage between them, in the event she needed to run.

"I'm Richard Grant."

Her fingers froze on the luggage handle as she quickly scanned the empty street. There was no one to save her. No one that would hear her scream. Her heart raced frantically as her eyes darted around for an escape.

The man held up his hands and stepped back. "I'm not here to hurt you. I'm here to help you."

Liar. She met Richard's gaze, trying to get a read on his energy to confirm her suspicion. Her gut screamed that she should run, yet...she was too stunned to move. He reached into his pocket, and her fingers tightened around the luggage handle.

"It's just a piece of paper," he said, slowly pulling it out of his pocket. He held out the document for her to take, yet she knew, just as soon as she did, the whacko would grab it and try to pull her into the alley and kill her dead.

His brows dipped so he unfolded it and held it up for her to see. A picture of Ryker's face was on the page. "Have you seen this man?"

Her gaze went to the paper and back to the man. She lifted her chin and squared her shoulders. No way was she making the same mistake again.

"No," she said firmly.

"We have reason to believe that he's been in contact with you."

Harper chewed her lip. "I talk to a lot of people and never know what they look like."

He smiled. "I know. You've talked to me."

Confusion clouded her mind. Why in the hell was he talking to her like a normal person and not some crazy psychopath? Hell, he seemed more normal than most of her family. "Are you here to kill me?"

His lip twisted for only a second. Humor filled his eyes before he masked it as he lowered his hand. "Why would you ask that?"

She shrugged. If she told him why,

he'd know she'd been talking to Ryker. "A hunch."

He handed her the paper and slid his hands back into his pocket. "Your hunches are normally better than that."

"It's been a long day," she said. Relief swarmed through her body as a yellow cab pulled up to the curb. "I have to go."

He nodded. "If you see Cage, run the other way. He's dangerous."

She pulled the door open to the cab as the driver put her bag in the trunk. She paused. "How so?"

"He's delusional." He pulled out a card and handed it to her. "Call me, if he shows."

She started to get in and then stopped. "Mr. Grant," she said, glancing down at the number on the card and then back up. "What does Cage want with me?"

"We're not sure why he's fixated on you. We just believe he is."

She started to get in and then stopped again. "What makes you think that? I mean there must have been something to make you assume that."

"He has a weird obsession with psychics. They normally end up dead, just like his sister-in-law. Are you sure he hasn't made contact yet?"

She shook her head. Not that she'd tell this guy anything. "I wouldn't know him if I passed him on the street."

His lips twitched. “If he does, call me, and I’ll help you.”

He gave a slight nod before he turned and walked away. Relief swished out of her body in the form of a sigh; the relief increasing the farther down the street he got without bothering to look back. She’d hadn’t been expecting that. She still had all of her body parts intact. What the hell had just happened?

“The meter’s running, lady. Are you coming or what?” the cabbie said, prompting her to get in the cab.

She mumbled her address to the driver and stared down at the card. Harper ran her finger over the embossed number, the card as cryptic as the man. No insignia, no name, just a single phone number. Since when did serial killers have business cards? Who was playing whom?

Chapter 8

Harper paid the cabbie and glanced up at her door. How in the hell was she going to act like nothing was wrong, knowing that Ryker could be watching? That was if he was even bothering to still watch. A mix of emotions rolled through her as she shoved her key in the door's lock and walked inside.

The smell of roses and chocolate drifted to her nose. Any other night, any other place, and she would have been happy. Instead, she leaned against the door and shoved the card into her pocket. The butterflies in her stomach danced, but she didn't know if it was in dread or delight.

"Harper?" Ryker called out, stepping

into the foyer. He'd changed since that morning, his shorts replaced with jeans. His shirt was now a deep blue, making the color of his eyes sparkle. He didn't make a move as the heat of his gaze slowly traveled down her body and back up. A look of uncertainty crossed his face.

"What are you doing here? Watching me from the cameras wasn't good enough?" she asked around the lump in her throat, unsure whom to trust.

"Your aunt and your sisters gave me the file. There was no way you would have known Grant was a fraud when he was talking to you."

Are you? The question crossed her mind and almost slipped from her lips.

Ryker's steps were slow and measured as he closed the distance between them. He cupped her cheek. "I'm sorry I hurt you."

She leaned into his palm and, for a brief second, let her eyes slip closed, not at all sure she should trust him. Her body reacted to him. Her brain recognized him. Her heart was starting to. What if everything she wanted to believe was wrong? Harper opened her eyes and met his gaze. Taking a deep, steadying breath, she gathered her resolve. "You were right. We can't do this."

His gaze searched hers as if looking for truth in her words. He didn't understand,

and she was afraid she wouldn't be able to make him without telling him about Grant's visit.

"What happened?"

She shook her head and stepped around him into the living room. Three dozen roses sat on the kitchen island, along with an assortment of various chocolate desserts. She picked up a brownie, broke it in half, and held it up to his mouth. She'd eat the other half only if he took a bite, unsure if Grant or he was really the one who wanted her dead.

Ryker bit into it and held her gaze. He knew. She could see it in his eyes, read it in his body. She waited for him to swallow before she took a single bite and put the brownie down. If she were going to die, it would be death by chocolate. There were worse ways to go.

"Why do you think Grant killed your sister-in-law?"

Ryker took an unconscious step back, and his features hardened. She knew she was pushing her luck, but she had to know for sure. "Why do you think he didn't?"

She held his gaze, matching the intensity in his eyes. She wasn't backing down until she had the answers she needed. The answers she deserved. "Always answering a question with a question. You ready to play a game?"

She was mentally calculating all of the sharp objects within her reach. She probably wouldn't win, but she'd die trying.

"Sure." His voice hardened. "Twenty Questions?" His eyes narrowed. "You can even go first."

Her stomach twisted in knots. Not because she thought he'd actually harm her, but because she didn't want Grant to be telling the truth. "Why do you think Grant killed her?"

"His fingerprints were in her house."

"He could have been there before. That doesn't mean he's a killer."

"My turn," he said, folding his arms over his chest. "What happened in the office today after I left?"

She breathed a sigh of relief. She could answer that one honestly without bringing up Grant. He'd happened outside the office. "I listened to the calls and tried to track Grant," she said as she moistened her lip.

"Is that all?"

"No. I drew a picture. My turn." She grabbed a bottle of wine from the fridge and poured a glass, leaving the thick bottle on the counter and within reaching distance. Thank God she hadn't bought the wine in a box. The answer to the next question would tell her whether or not he was lying. "Was your sister-in-law psychic?"

His mouth had parted before he snapped it closed. Her question startled him. "Why would you ask that?"

"Answer the question." Her heart raced, and her shoulders tightened. It was now or never.

"Yes," he said. His words eased her shoulders.

"Why didn't you tell me?"

He shook his head. "You skipped my turn." He grabbed the counter and met her gaze. "Who told you that?"

Harper slipped the card out of her pocket and slid it across the counter. "The same man you're convinced wants me dead. I don't know what sick game he and you are playing, but I really wish you'd leave me out of it."

Ryker picked up the card, and she grabbed the wine glass and the bottle before walking into her bedroom, closing the door behind her. She leaned on the wood and tried to calm her erratic heartbeat. She needed the space. Time to re-gather her resolve. She let out a shaky breath. One of these men wanted her dead.

A knock sounded at her back, making her jump.

"Harper." Ryker's voice had softened. "Did he hurt you?"

"No." She stepped away from the door.

"And I think you need to leave."

The doorknob twisted and slowly opened until he was staring at her. "Not a chance in hell. Harper, he knows who you are."

Her legs bumped the bed as she slowly backed away. "He said you're delusional. He said I shouldn't trust you, or I'll end up dead."

Ryker's hand stayed on the knob, and he didn't make a move to come any closer. "You believe him?"

Her breath raced as shame, anger, and frustration heated her cheeks. "I don't want to believe him."

Anguish crossed his face before he quickly masked the regret in his eyes. "Do you still have the pepper spray and my knife?"

She nodded. "Yeah, do I need it?"

"Get them and meet me in the SUV." With those words, he turned and walked away. For the second time today, she was left confused. Harper quickly pushed the haze away, not waiting to make sense of it.

"I'm not going anywhere with you, Ryker."

Ryker paused in the hallway and turned back to face her. "Your sisters told me today that I should believe in you. That I should trust you, and I do. This is *me* trusting *you*. This is one of those pivotal moments in life, when your decision will define where we go from here. Once I walk out that door, if you're not with me, I'm not coming back. You either trust me, or you don't."

She stood motionless. She wanted to scream that she did, and yet the words wouldn't come out. Goosebumps rose on her arms as she mentally debated. Did she trust him?

He gave a hard nod and turned, walking away.

Her heart clenched tight, making it unbearable to breathe. "Ryker, wait."

He didn't.

She barely had time to jump into the passenger seat as he put the SUV in reverse.

Chapter 9

"Where are we?" she asked, staring up at the huge brick warehouse downtown.

"You'll see." He turned off the ignition and got out, and she was quick to follow. She'd passed this building a million times before, but she had absolutely no idea what was inside. There were no signs on the building, nothing to indicate what she was walking into. Would they even find her dead body inside?

Ryker slid his key into the lock and punched some numbers on a security pad before he shut and locked the door again. "This is me."

She glanced around the bottom floor of the empty industrial building. "Did you decorate yourself?"

A smile split his lips as he led her to the elevator and hit the button. "You're the only person, besides Eve and my brother, that I've brought here."

Harper stepped on the elevator and glanced up at the cameras in the corners. This guy had security on steroids. Even those steroids had steroids. Images of a movie she'd once seen drifted through her mind, where the woman was pinned to the elevator wall. Her grin grew wider, unable to shake the naughty thoughts of being with the dangerous man.

"I'm guessing you've never had sex on this elevator. Because you know, that would just be...naughty." Bend her over and slap her ass kinky.

"Are you offering?" He reached for the emergency button.

Yes. "No." She stepped off of the elevator into a foyer. A beautiful painting hung on the wall. The trees looked similar to the ones she'd drawn. Only these were in sharp, vivid colors of greens and brown, and hers were in ink blue. "You have a painting. I wouldn't have ever guessed you had an eye for art."

He ran his hand over the dried paint. "I don't. Eve painted this for me."

"It's beautiful." Her heart clenched in sadness. Pain reflected in his eyes as he stared at the trees.

"Behind the trees," she whispered.

"What did you say?" he asked.

"The memory stick Grant was looking for. I'd said it was behind the trees." She slipped the folded picture out of her pocket and handed it to him. "Similar to these, but different. Did Eve paint more?"

He unfolded the picture and smiled at her makeshift drawing. "This is what you drew today?"

"Yeah. I'm no artist, but I was trying to recall what I saw when I said behind the trees."

He grabbed Harper and swung her around, the smile on his face ginormous.

"Whoa there, big fella. I want off this merry-go-round."

"I could kiss you." He slowed and sat her down. "The picture you drew is one of her paintings." He pointed to the lone flower behind the clump of trees. "She must have hidden it behind the painting."

Okayyyy. She walked farther into his place. "Before we run off, will you at least tell me why you brought me to your secret bat-cave."

"I'm no hero," he said, walking past her.

"Villain lair? Do villains have lairs, or arc they called hideouts?"

He turned and lifted his brow.

"What? You look like a guy who would know." She followed him, gazing around the room, one side livable and the other looked like a picture straight out of spy novel. There was a rack of guns and sharp, pointy things along one wall. "That's an accident waiting to happen. Or fate." She shrugged. "Haven't you ever seen the movie *Final Destination*?"

"No."

"Not a big movie fan." She pointed to the wall of monitors. The pictures on the screen were of inside her house and around her property. She felt violated and a little turned on. "You must be into reality TV. So, this is what you've been watching?"

"Don't worry, you didn't pick your nose." He chuckled.

She shrugged. "Could be worse. I like to dance naked, and I have absolutely no rhythm."

"I would have paid to see that." He moved to the monitors and stroked a few more buttons, making the pictures on the screens change to the front of her office building. He sat in the chair and rewound the video to the point he saw Harper locking the office door and pulling her suitcase. He stopped and hit Play.

"That's Grant," she said, gesturing to the man talking to her on the street.

"No, it's not." He clicked a few more buttons, and a face appeared on another screen that looked nothing like the man she'd spoken to. "That's Grant."

"Well, who the hell is that?" she asked pointing to the man showing her Ryker's picture.

"My brother," he said, pushing away from the computer. He turned in the chair and rested his hands on her hips. "He's more dangerous than I am, Harper. I need to know if you told him about me or about giving Grant my sister in law's location."

"I said I don't know you, and that I wouldn't recognize you if I passed you on the street." Her eyes searched his as a sinking feeling rested in the pit of her stomach. "Why?"

"He blames me for her death. The fact I encouraged her to use her abilities. He'll do anything to get back at me, including killing you so that I will feel his pain."

Talk about overkill, but she was sure grief made normal people do strange and deranged things.

"He had his chance." She gestured to the screen. "Why didn't he take it?"

Ryker shrugged. "I'm not sure what his plan is, unless he's waiting to do it in front of me, or maybe he hasn't put all the pieces together."

"And I thought my family was nuts. I'm pretty sure yours takes first prize."

"Yours is still nuts, in a dipped-in-sugar kind of way. Mine's just dipped in arsenic instead. Let me just say that my family is the reason I'm good at my job.

You come from a long line of psychics; I come from a long line of not-so-nice people, only I took the legal path."

"I'll bet you didn't bring many girls home."

He dropped his gaze. She could tell when he was keeping something from her. He was quiet without any quips. He looked like a boy who had lost his childhood dog.

"Eve was my best friend. I brought her home and introduced her to my brother. It was love at first sight and they married within 6 months. I was happy for them, you know. The women in our lives don't tend to stick around long when they see the real us. Eve was different. She was a sweet soul, trying to make us whole."

"She sounds like someone I would have instantly liked." Harper gave him a sad smile. He rose from his spot and cupped her cheek. The electricity between them sizzled from his touch.

"She already liked you." He smiled. "You've talked to her too."

"I don't understand."

"My company was courting her, like Grant was using you. She had premonitions they were doing unethical things, and she couldn't bring herself to commit."

"Do *you* think they were doing anything unethical?"

He pinched his lips together. "Yeah, I do. I worked in security for them. I was trained to detect any outside threats, but I would have never guessed that the people I worked for were the dangerous ones. When she brought it up, I started paying closer attention and piecing things together, but we didn't have enough to prove it." He cleared his throat. "Anyway, you told her you got a bad vibe from the offer and the location, so she declined, but couldn't let things rest."

"I'm sorry."

"Don't be. She was stubborn, just like you. She wanted my help proving what she'd seen, but knew no one would believe her, so I offered to help her find the evidence. She was getting information from other sources too, but she wouldn't tell me who. I encouraged her. That was the first of a lot of bad ideas I'd given her, including coming clean with her family. They practically disowned her. I guess you could say I started her on this path. I promised to help her bring down the company I worked for, and when the dust settled, I told her I'd help her try and buy into yours. She just wanted to be happy, Harper, and I wanted to be the one to give it to her since her own family turned out to be douche bags."

"How did Grant figure out she had a memory drive, and why does he want it?"

Ryker shrugged. “I’m not sure unless he was the other source she mentioned that was giving her information. All I know is the guy claimed to be psychic when he was actually a fraud. He used Eve and you to help get through his assignments. Why he was there to begin with, is as much a mystery as to how he knew about the memory drive. The day she called and claimed to have what we needed is the day she died and he went missing. His fingerprints were found at Eve’s place.”

Harper’s eyes searched his when he rested his hand on her hip. “And what about your brother?”

“My brother.” Ryker sighed. “I thought I was doing Eve a favor. I promised to protect her. He blames me for her death, and he should. I blame myself. I ruined her life in more ways than one. She lost her family and her life because of me.”

She wrapped her arms around his waist and rested her head on his chest. “Families can suck. But you didn’t kill her any more than I did. We aren’t the monsters responsible, but I’m going to help you shine light into the darkness of the person who did.”

“If my brother doesn’t kill you first.” He kissed the top of her head.

“If your brother doesn’t kill me first.” She glanced up at him with a lopsided grin. “I know how to help.” Her smile grew as excitement coiled through her veins. "You want to know exactly what happened to your sister-in-law and who killed her? I can tell you. It's just going to be a bit tricky."

"I can do tricky, and I can keep you alive, if you just trust me."

"I do," she said, meaning it with every fiber of her being.

Ryker kissed her long and hard, lifting her into his arms. His tongue dove between her lips, tasting and teasing. Her legs straddled his waist as his hands cupped the globes of her ass.

"I have a few other tricks I'd like to show you first."

"Tricks can be good." She grinned. "I can tie a knot in a cherry stem with just my tongue."

"What else can you do with that tongue?" he asked, and turning from the computers, he carried her down the hall.

He took her into a bedroom and kept her mouth too busy for her to even look around. Not that she cared. She was much more interested in what he had to offer than in her surroundings, although knowing there were no knives hanging from the ceiling might put her at more ease. She broke the kiss. "Anything in here that can hurt me?"

He grinned. The bulge in his pants grew harder. "I'll be gentle."

Harper slowly slid down his body to her feet as he kissed her again, walking her backward. Her legs bumped the bed, and he followed her down, not for a minute giving her time to change her mind. His hands were all over her. His body on top of hers.

"What is with you and always wearing clothes?" His grin turned wicked. He grabbed the hem of her shirt and kissed her stomach as he slowly moved it up her body and over her head. His hand rested on her rib cage below her bra. His gaze held hers as he lowered his lips to heat her skin.

She didn't allow herself to think, to analyze how he made her feel or the chaos that surrounded them being together. It didn't matter in that minute; only he and she mattered in that minute. The times she'd spent fantasizing about this man couldn't compare to his touch, to his taste, to him.

Harper raked her nails over his shoulders, earning a grin as he slid her bra straps down her shoulders. "You're going to kill me with anticipation."

"We're not in a hurry. We've got the rest of the night."

He'd drive her mad before he ever got her completely undressed. She pulled his shirt, by the collar, over his head and tossed it on the floor. The sight of his impressive chest was enough to make her mouth water. She wanted to taste every inch of him. "We've had months of foreplay."

His smile grew as she helped him along. Arching her back, she unhooked her bra and reached for her zipper. His hands covered hers and brushed them out of the way. He took his time, slowly sliding her jeans and panties down her legs. His gaze heated her skin as his hands slowly moved up her thighs.

She clenched her legs closed, effectively cutting him off. If he touched her now, she'd go up in flames, and it would all be over before it even began. She tsked. "Your turn."

"With pleasure." Ryker slid off the bed and she watched, mesmerized, as he undressed, taking his time like a stripper working to heighten the anticipation.

"I was right. You're an assassin stripper, aren't you?"

His laughter was deep. Amusement touched his eyes as he dropped his jeans. No boxers in sight. His massive size was enough to snare her gaze, and she was hard-pressed to look away.

"Oh...a commando assassin stripper. You sure do have a big...gun. That should be your new title."

He crawled up on the bed and spread her legs, resting between her thighs.

"Treasure hunter fits better. I'm about to search for yours."

She took his cock in hand and gave it a firm stroke before rubbing it through her folds and aligning him up. She was already hot and ready for him. "Let me draw you a map."

He slid inside and stole her ability to speak. She moaned as he moved slowly in and out. Lowering his head, he kissed her lips. It wasn't going to take long. She was already on the edge. Every thrust sent tingles along her nerve endings, and pleasure zipped through her body.

Harper slowly slid her nails down his back and wrapped her legs around his waist. He surged in deeper, harder, and with more haste. That was how she wanted him. With nothing but desire driving his force.

He moved like a man without thought, only need, searing every nerve in her body to life. Their quick pants filled the room, the slick slide of his body against hers brought her to the edge. She didn't want it to stop. She didn't want it to end, but she could feel it building inside, her channel tightening around him, bringing him to the frenzied need she felt.

He held her gaze and reached between their bodies. "You're going before me."

She didn't have time to respond as he circled her clit and pressed her home.

His name broke free from her lips as her orgasm hit. She pierced him with her nails as he moved, once, then twice more and stilled deep inside. His groan was her reward.

He lowered his head to the juncture of her neck as their hearts started to slow. "I didn't use a condom."

"I'm on the pill," she breathed out. "And I don't sleep around."

He raised his head. "I know."

He rolled and pulled her against his chest. "I like you without clothes. We need to change the dress code."

****

Ryker woke before Harper. He pulled her close to his body, enjoying the feel of her in his arms. The way she molded against his skin. Last night he'd taken her two more times before she'd fallen asleep from exhaustion, and even now his body was awake to say hello. His cock pressed against her ass as he moved his hand up to cup her breast.

"You're insatiable," she said, rolling onto her back.

"You bring it out in me." His hand rested on her stomach as he leaned down and kissed her. His warm palm had slowly moved down the juncture of her thighs when he heard a sound. His fingers froze, and he broke the kiss.

"Why are you stopping?" she whispered.

"Shh." He turned his head toward the direction of the door when he heard the noise again. He slid from the bed and slipped into his jeans. He hit the button on the headboard. The headboard opened, revealing the secret hiding spot where he kept his favorite guns. He grabbed one and slid the chamber open, making sure it was loaded.

"Stay here."

Harper sat up and pulled the sheet up around her body. She had a right to the worry shining in her eyes. Hell, he was sure it showed in his.

He eased the door open, cringing when it creaked, and he peered down the hall. He glanced back once more to find Harper getting dressed before he slipped out into the hall. His ears strained to hear a sound. Something to give him an indication of who or what might be in his house and how they'd managed to enter without tripping the alarm.

"His car is downstairs, so he's probably still sleeping." The voice of his housekeeper, Rosemary, made his shoulders relax as he rounded the corner into the living room.

His entire body froze when he spotted his brother staring at the computer monitors. Ryker lifted his gun and aimed at his brother's head. "What are you doing here?"

Eric glanced over his shoulder and lifted a brow. "I knew she was lying. Where is she?"

Chapter 10

"What the hell are you talking about?" Ryker asked, trying to play innocent. There was no way his brother could even fathom that Ryker had made contact.

Rosemary backed out of the living room. "I'm sorry, Mr. Cage. He's your brother. I thought it would be okay."

Ryker nodded and never lowered his gun. "It's okay, but you need to leave, Rosemary."

She quickly nodded and hurried out of sight.

"Why did you send that woman to the hotel to kill me?" Ryker growled.

"What the fuck are you talking about?

I wouldn't have a woman do my dirty work."

His answer caught Ryker off guard. If it hadn't been his brother, then it had to be Grant, but how had he figured out where Ryker was staying?

Eric turned to Ryker, his arms crossed over his chest. "I know she's here. Where is she?"

"How would I know?" he asked.

Eric's lips twitched. "You're still aiming your gun at me. Did you think you're the only one who could hack her system? I know about the calls. Eve's, Grant's, and yours. I've listened to them. I know she's responsible." His brows dipped in anger. "So where the fuck is she!"

Fuck. "You'll have to kill me to get to her."

"Fine." Eric lifted his Glock and pointed it at Ryker's head.

His heart raced. His finger on the trigger.

"No. Wait," Harper said from behind. "It's not his fault. Don't kill him."

Eric's gun wavered between Ryker and Harper as if not sure who he'd kill first.

"What are you doing, Harper? I told you to stay," He said, unwilling to take his eyes off Eric.

Harper cleared her throat. "Do your homework. That won't ever work with me." She lifted her hands as if to show him she was unarmed and took a tentative step toward Eric. Ryker pulled her back just as the elevator dinged, arriving back to the floor.

He heard Betty's voice before he caught a glimpse of turquoise hair. "Brotherly love at its best."

Eric's gun swayed between Harper, Betty, and him. She had her own gun pointed at Eric. "Everyone has five seconds to lower their weapons, or I'm going to be using your balls as target practice."

"Who the hell are you?" Eric asked.

"One. Two."

Harper shoved Ryker's gun to aim at the ground. "She means it."

"Three. Four." Harper rushed to Eric and lowered his gun before letting out a shaky breath. "Whoa, that was close. Everyone still has their swimmers."

The elevator dinged again, and he heard Harper's sisters' voices in the hall. Cooper appeared around the corner first with his gun drawn. "Are we too late?"

"Oh, for the love of God, you guys need to move out of my way," Quinn shouted before Cara, Becca, Grace and she appeared in the room.

"Who are they?" Eric asked Ryker.

"We're one big, happy, fucking family," Quinn said, moving to Harper's side. "No one is dying today unless it's by my hands."

"We're here to settle this once and for all," Cara said, holding her belly.

"Who the fuck are you?" Eric growled.

"Harper's sisters," Ryker answered. "They're her family, every God-lovin' one of them."

"No' yet," Ian added as he rested his arm on Becca's shoulders.

"Not ever." Becca shrugged it off and hit his abs, making Ian grunt.

Quinn stepped up on her toes and kissed Collin's lips. "Sweetie, be a dear and order us a pizza."

"It's eight in the morning, lass. I'm not sure anyone delivers."

"Your baby wants pizza," she said in a deep, guttural voice. One that would suggest her head would start spinning next.

"Pizza it is," Collin said and knocked Ian on the shoulder. "You're riding with me." He paused and glanced at Coop. "You got this?"

Coop nodded. "I've got it."

"Ohhh, and mint ice cream with pickles," Cara added.

Harper shrugged her shoulders at Eric. "Hormones. What are you going to do?"

"I'll tell you what we're going to do," Quinn said, walking straight up to Eric and slipping the gun from his fingers.

"We're going to handle this like adults, and we're going to tell you once and for all what happened to Eve."

"How?" Eric growled.

Cara walked over to him and held out her hand. "I'm sorry about Eve, but I need her wedding band."

"What makes you think I have it on me?" he asked, glancing at Ryker.

"It's better not to ask," Ryker said, moving to stand behind Harper. He watched as Eric slid out his wallet and dug inside for the ring.

"I told you to stay," Ryker whispered in Harper's ear.

"And let you get killed?" she asked glancing sideways at him. She kissed his cheek. "I think I'm entitled to a few more nights like the last one because of all your highly inappropriate calls."

Eric slid the ring from his wallet and handed it to Cara. The way she took the ring and closed her eyes. The way Cooper moved closer to her as if he was afraid of what she might see.

"She can see the important memories. They're like flashes of a movie."

Cara bit her lip, a look of worry on her face. "I…." She paused and snapped her mouth closed. Ryker had a feeling about what she was seeing and held his breath. If she'd said that out loud, he would definitely be dying today, and rightly so.

He'd tried to talk Eve out of the marriage. Tried to warn her against his family.

Cara cleared her throat. "Yes, well....okay." She let out a long breath. "She was in the kitchen and about to take off her ring, but a knock on the door stopped her." Cara took several deep breaths. "The man at the door, dark hair, dark eyes, dressed in a black T-shirt and fatigues. Commando looking," she amended. "He rushed her with a knife as soon the door opened. She didn't even have time to say a word. He stabbed her in the stomach and twisted the knife. There was so much blood." Cara's body sagged. "She fell to the ground, and he squatted down beside her and said *I'm going to kill every one of you freaks and send you all back to hell.*"

Cara shook her head.

"He has a tattoo on his arm. It looks military in nature. He has a scar on his face near his left eye. He looks familiar, but I don't know from where." Cara gasped. "He picked up a picture and dropped it to the floor crushing it with his boot." Cara slowly shook her head. "Where have I seen him?" She held her hand to her belly as if in protective mode.

"Cara," Cooper said, moving closer. "Open your eyes."

She shook her head. "I need to remember his face."

"Baby," he said, holding out his hand as if he was about to touch her. "You've done enough."

He took hold of her arm, and she sagged against his body, drained.

"Fatigues?" Eric asked, running his hand through his hair.

"Grant doesn't wear fatigues," Ryker said, moving to the computer. He pulled up a picture of Grant and glanced at Cara. "Is this the guy?"

Cara shook her head. "No. That's not him. Not even close." Cara glanced at Quinn. "I need our sketch artist."

Ryker pulled up a group of several men, from his company, who had been involved in the project on one screen and a group of several men and women on another screen. "How about any of these?"

Cara moved closer to the screen. Minutes ticked by as her gaze traveled over the faces. She shook her head. "None of them."

"Fuck," Eric growled and lowered his head.

Cara handed him back the ring. "I'm sorry."

Eric opened his wallet to put the ring back inside, and Cara grabbed it. Her breath hitched as she pointed to a picture with Eric, Ryker, Eve, and Eve's step-brother. "Him. Who is he?"

Chapter 11

Eric's brows dipped as he met Ryker's gaze. He handed the wallet to Ryker. "Are you sure?"

She nodded. "He's the killer."

Ryker's fingers started flying across the screen, and the picture in Eric's wallet appeared larger on the screen. "You're sure?"

"I'm positive. Who is he?"

"He's Eve's stepbrother, Norman," Eric said as the rest of the sisters moved closer to the screen. "Military trained in explosives and electronics."

"I know that face," Grace, the youngest Thatcher, said.

The other sisters crowded the desk.

"I do too," Becca added.

"What does Norman do?" Quinn asked.

"He works with computers now," Eric answered.

"For the company I work for," Ryker added.

Cara pointed to the screen. "He's the guy that's installing our new system. He's the one we contracted with."

"Shit." Harper grabbed Eric's gun and hurried to the elevator, slamming her finger on the button. "He's there now. He has a damn key."

Ryker flew out of his chair and grabbed her before she could get on the elevator. "Calm down."

Harper's eyes widened as she struggled in his hold. "I've got to stop him."

"We will, after we see what's he's doing," Ryker said, only releasing his hold when she stopped struggling. "I've got video, or have you forgotten?"

He took Harper's hand and pulled her back into the room. He sat down at the computer, and within seconds, the security video feed was up on the screen. The building's lights were on, each screen void of a person. He continued flicking through the screens until he caught movement. "There."

Harper held her hand clutched to her

heart as she watched Norman in her office. He was going through her drawers and grinned when he spotted the Scotch. He pulled it out and drank half the bottle before throwing it at the window into the hall. The glass shattered.

Ryker rose and moved to the back of the room, watching Eric at the elevator. He knew that look; he knew what Eric was about to do. Getting away from this bunch would be the hardest. He shook his head and grabbed his gun. He gestured toward the emergency stairs and followed behind his brother. They had work to do.

****

Harper glanced around the room. Her heart raced when she found Eric and Ryker gone. Aunt Betty held out her keys. "Use the chair."

"What chair?"

Aunt Betty grinned. "You'll see."

"Oh no, you aren't going anywhere," Quinn growled. "If those two maniacs want to walk into danger, that's one thing, but don't think for a minute that I'm going to let you walk out that door."

"I have to," Harper said and took Aunt Betty's gun in passing. "I can't let them go to jail, or worse, die. They've been through enough."

"You aren't thinking clearly," Cara

said, taking a step in Harper's direction as the elevator door opened. "We'll go with you. We'll call the police."

She shook her head and stepped into the elevator. "You have more than yourself to worry about, and it would kill me if something happened to the baby or you." Harper hit the button to the ground floor and held her sister's gaze as the door slid closed, cutting off her view.

****

Five minutes later, Harper pulled the door open to her building. She bypassed the elevator and took the stairs to camouflage her arrival. The stairwell lights illuminated her path as she climbed the stairs, letting adrenaline be her guiding force. She peered through the little window in the door to find the lights on her floor were off. Her heart raced as she held the gun steady. She reached for the door with shaky hands and eased it open. A single light was flashing from her office as Harper stepped forward. Her foot caught on something and she glanced down.

Grant was on the ground in a pool of blood that was soaking into the floor. She squatted, placing her fingers on his neck. A slight pulse.

Harper ducked into Quinn's old office

and grabbed the phone from the desk before ducking behind it. She lifted the receiver and held it to her ear. No dial tone, no way to call for help.

Harper put the gun on the desk and eased back out into the hall. Slipping her hands beneath Grant's arms, she eased him into Quinn's office and out of view. Frantically she searched for something to stop the blood. Nothing.

She slipped her shirt off and pressed it to the open wound. Her only chance at getting help was in her office. She rose and grabbed the gun. Ducking beneath windows, she moved to where the light was. Straining to hear, she leaned against the wall, the gun held against her chest. Nothing.

She eased over the broken glass to peer inside the room. It was empty. She hurried inside, grabbed a piece of paper, scribbled the words *Call 911*, and held it up to the security camera. She hoped that her sisters were still watching.

She left it on the desk for her sisters and moved back outside the room. She quickly worked her way through the offices; not a single soul was in sight. The door to the roof stood open. Fear and desperation coursed through her veins as she eased up each step, trying not to make a sound. She strained to hear words, noises, anything that would tell her what was waiting. The door to the roof stood open. There was no noise, no sound, nothing. She eased outside, and her breath caught. Eric and Ryker were lying on the ground.

She dropped the gun by Eric's prone body and felt for a pulse in his neck. He was still breathing. She quickly moved to Ryker, and he, too, was still alive; a tear slipped down her cheek. His eyes slid open, but his words were garbled. "He's rigged the place to blow. You need to get out."

Her body froze and tears filled her eyes. She couldn't leave him. She couldn't take the chance that Norman would wait until the office was full of people to hurt.

"I can't." She pressed a kiss to his lips and rose. Ryker caught her hand.

"Please," he begged.

"Don't you dare die on me. Help is coming. I have to warn them," she whispered for the world to hear and slipped her fingers free. She jogged back to the steps and down them, back onto her office floor, the gun held tightly in her hands.

The energy in the building was worse than the feeling she had gotten when Ryker had mentioned a meeting in Mexico several days prior. This energy was worse than any energy she'd felt before. It was black and dark and suffocating. A ghost appeared in the hall, startling her. The Highlander with the red beard was donning his sword and pointing down the corridor.

"He's down there?" she whispered, earning her a grin. Harper ran into her office, wrote the word *BOMB* in big letters and held it up to the video. She let out a shaky breath and went in the one direction Ryker and her sisters would kill her for, if they knew. She was walking straight into harm's way. She had no choice but to stop him before he blew the place up.

She eased down the corridor, the Highlander showing her the way. He drifted through the stairwell door that led to the basement. She eased it open, the gun pointed at the floor as she slowly descended the stairs. She didn't have a plan. She hadn't a clue what she was doing. She knew one thing. If this building collapsed, Ryker was going to die.

She stopped on the last step and heard a man whistling. She glanced around the corner and found Norman squatted down with his back to her. She couldn't see what he was doing. She had no clue how to diffuse a bomb. She eased around the corner with the gun held in both hands. Her gaze darted around the room and landed on one of the old chairs they had stored just a week ago. Aunt

Betty's words came rushing back. *Use the chair.* Why would she need to use a damn chair when she had a gun? Harper sidestepped around a chair and shoved the barrel up to his head. "Rise, nice and slow."

The whistling ceased as the man rose. "Which one are you?"

"The one you pissed off."

Norman raised his hands. Some type of device was clutched in his grasp as he turned to face her. "Harper." His lips twisted in a smile.

"Where's the bomb?" she demanded.

His smile grew. "If I push this button, the whole building blows."

She aimed the gun at his leg, and her hands shook as she pulled the trigger.

Norman fell to his side and gripped his leg with one hand while holding the trigger in the other.

"You're a surprise." He lay on the floor and lifted the detonator in his hand. "The other three were easy pickings when I shot them. You, on the other hand, I hadn't counted on."

"You shouldn't have drunk my scotch."

He chuckled. His body shook, and he immediately winced.

"You killed Eve."

He lifted his brow. "I'm going to kill you too."

"Why her?"

"I was working with her to try and tear that company apart from the inside out. I was one of the people feeding her the information to help bring those bastards down, and how does she fucking repay me? She admits to being a damn psychic and that you were the one who confirmed that working for the company was a bad decision."

"Why Richard Grant? What was his part in all this?"

"He was an ex-cop turned private detective that she hired to get a first-hand look at what exactly was going on inside. She said she'd help him to make the other's think he was legit." Richard narrowed his eyes. "When she told me that Grant and she were both your clients, that's when I realized there was a bigger infestation. Taking down the organization was going to be a piece of cake, but it wouldn't stop the corruption. It wouldn't stop your company from spreading its evil."

"If Richard knew about the memory drive, why would he call me and ask where it was hidden? Your story doesn't make sense."

Norman grinned, his eyes sparkled. "I might have suggested that Ryker killed Eve in an attempt to stop her from outing his company, and Richard bought it. The dumb son of a bitch actually bought it."

"And you think we're evil? You need to look in the mirror, buddy. You have it written all over your ugly mug." Harper held the gun steady, deciding what body part to shoot next. Which one wouldn't have him pushing the button? She could only think of two: his head or his hand. He couldn't push the button if he had no fingers. "Give me the remote."

"Come get it," he growled, trying to push himself to stand.

She didn't think about her next action; she couldn't. She aimed for his hand and pulled the trigger. Her eyes might have closed as she shot, but she'd never admit it. Not when she hit the target. The remote went flying across the room as blood exploded from his hand.

"You bitch." He lowered his head and rammed it into her stomach. Her legs caught on the chair, tripping her and sending them both crashing to the ground. The force of his body, and the fall, stole the breath from her lungs. The chair had toppled over next to her and the gun flew from her hand. Norman was on top of her as she squirmed beneath him and rolled to her stomach, the stairs in her view. Blood dripped from his hand as he closed his other fingers around her neck. "It's time for you to die."

She reached for the gun. It was too far away. She struggled to breathe as she squirmed beneath him. His body pinned her down. Her fingers closed around the chair. She grabbed it with both hands and rolled, bringing the force of the wooden chair against his head and knocking him off balance. The impact left him dazed and she struggled to her feet. The sirens were loud outside, the police calling from above.

“Down here.” She yelled louder, “We’re down here.” Hope welled up in her body as footsteps ran down the steps and officers appeared in the room. They held him at gunpoint, and Harper dropped to her knees letting the gun slip from her fingers. “There’s three with gunshot wounds. Two on the roof and one in an office on the third floor.”

Chapter 12

A month and a half went by, and all three men recovered. The hidden computer drive was found, and it was Ryker, Eric, and Richard Grant's faces splashed in the tabloids for everyone to see as the men were credited for leaking the corruption. A picture of Eve flashed on the TV, and Harper's heart clenched. She was the reason Harper's life had turned upside down. Eve had been a casualty, just like Harper. Norman was sitting in a psych ward recovering from his ordeal. The bomb squad had removed the bomb without incident, and Harper's sisters....well, they were left dealing with questions from the media about their involvement. *Did a spirit tell you? Was it a premonition? Who's going to be the next president?*

The phones were ringing off the hook now. Calls from TV producers and celebrities. One from a network that wanted to tell their story. It tripled their annual revenue in less than a month. Each day she spent dealing with the aftermath, and each night, Ryker found a delicious way to help her unwind.

Harper adjusted the Bluetooth in her ear. This day was a long time coming.

"What are you wearing?" Ryker asked into the headset, his voice as silky and smooth as the first day they'd spoken.

"A dress," she answered and toyed with the satin between her fingers. "Did you sign the papers?"

"Yes. I kept my promise. The company is yours. Are you getting cold feet?"

She smiled at his question. For a hit man/mob boss/stripper, he sounded awfully unsure of himself. "I was just debating my options. A life with an unemployed, commando stripper wasn't one I dreamed of as a little girl."

"Don't you mean treasure hunter? Is that better?"

"Well, when you put it that way," she said with a smile. "I've got a treasure you can find."

"I plan to spend a lifetime finding it over and over again. I love you, Harper."

"I love you too, Ryker Cage. Oh, and before I forget...Thank you for not making me a statistic."

"You are a statistic." He chuckled. "We're going to be one of those couples that live happily ever after."

"That makes us a fairytale," she corrected.

"Well, you are my princess," he said. "Now get your ass down here. We have a room full of guests waiting to watch me make an honest woman out of you."

"Don't you mean watch me make an honest man out of you?"

"Now who's dreaming?" He chuckled.

"Ten," she said as she sauntered across the room and grabbed her bouquet.

"Ten what?"

"Ten minutes is the amount of time it's going to take before I kiss your lips. Ten minutes and you're going to be mine."

"Time starts now."

The End.

I hope you enjoyed Harper's story. Keep reading for a sneak peek at Grace's journey.

Chapter 1

Grace bounced her crossed leg as she flipped impatiently through a magazine in the dating agency office. Why was she here? As a favor of course. Why else would anyone wait thirty minutes beyond an appointment time just to be matched with some losers? She had a job she loved, a family that loved her back, and she could get any man she set her mind on. She needed a dating agency service much like she needed to rub honey all over her body and stand atop an anthill. Neither promised a good time. And yet, here she sat with a room full of women looking for love. They'd have better chances by calling Linked Inc. At least the psychics that worked for her would be more accurate.

Maybe she should leave some business cards near the magazines.

The clock ticking on the wall grated on her nerves and taunted the precious time she'd never get back. The unease in the room was thick and choking. The only person speaking was the receptionist on a personal call. Unprofessional, check, check. And this company claimed to have a ninety-eight percent success rate in the first match. What a load of…

The door across the room opened, cutting off Grace's thought. A woman in her sixties wearing a polyester suit and her hair up in a tight bun gave Grace a pinched smile. "Ms. Thornton?"

Finally. Grace tossed the magazine aside and grabbed her purse. If she'd been forced to wait another ten minutes she'd have to go back to her best friend, Chloe, without any answers. Grace followed behind the lady while fighting the nerves in her stomach from flipping. She could do this. She was undercover. A female version of James Bond. Maybe she should have brought her Tazer. That might have made the wait more entertaining.

The woman stopped and gestured to an office. "If you'll take a seat, Mr. Stone will be in shortly. He's just finishing up his meeting."

Grace walked into the room and turned to thank the lady to find that the door was already closed and the woman had vanished ninja-style, leaving Grace alone in the big corner office. If that woman worked for Grace, she'd buy her a pair of squeaky shoes and a bell for Christmas and probably be reported to HR for targeting seniors.

Expensive cologne teased her nose. The dark cherry wood and leather furnishings made the room feel like her father's home office. She should have sat as she'd been instructed. She never did follow instructions.

Grace walked around the room, running her finger over the polished bookshelf. Not a dust speck in sight. She moved to the pictures on the wall. Several diplomas and awards were displayed for the infamous Sam Stone. The guy was book smart to her street smart. They were going to get along like peanut butter and spinach.

She walked to the desk. Neat and tidy. Nothing for her to even snoop through. This guy was boring, but the view was fantastic. Grace stood in front of the window and glanced over at Linked Inc.'s building. Her office sat directly facing his. Her blinds were open; the room was dark. This would be the perfect place to spy on her sisters. If she still did that kind of thing.

"Do you like the view?"

She swiveled around to find tall, dark, and yummy in a black Armani suit standing in the room. The enemy. A smile split her lips as she let her gaze travel down his body and back up, making him feel as ridiculous as she did for even agreeing to this cockamamie scheme. "I do now."

His lip twitched as he closed the door behind him. "One of the Thornton five. I never thought I'd see the day."

Ohh. He'd heard of her. Score one point for him. She was totally keeping tally.

"I see you've done your research, Mr. Stone."

"I like to know my neighbors."

"Tell me, what else do you know?" she asked, moving back around the desk to sit in one of the chairs, crossing her legs seductively. A total Sharon Stone move. His gaze followed the movement. So he wasn't gay like Chloe had heard through the grape vine. Score one for Grace. She could work with that.

"I take my job seriously, Ms. Thornton, and I must admit you checked all the right boxes on the application, although you'll have to forgive me for not taking you at your word. Successful, beautiful, you're not in a relationship, and you're a medium. I think that sums it up."

"Sharp-tongued, smartass, hates animals. Which part bothers you most?"

"We aren't here to discuss me." He cleared his throat and took his seat. He leaned back in his chair, the leather creaking under his weight, and steepled his fingers. His gaze never left hers. The move was one she'd expect from a principal or therapist. If her principal had been as good looking as this enemy, she might have skipped more and been one of the perpetual problem kids. She wouldn't have minded sitting in his office all day. "What I'd like to know is, why are you here?"

"To find Mr. Right." She smiled brightly. The answer came as quickly as she'd rehearsed. "Isn't that why everyone comes here?"

"You don't strike me as the kind of woman who needs my services. We serve three categories of women. The shy ones who have a hard time meeting someone. The kind that is tired of falling for the wrong men, and the ones looking for a rebound without putting in the effort of finding a match for themselves. You don't fit into one of those boxes. So let's be honest here. I can't help you unless I know what I'm up against. Why is it *you* can't find Mr. Right?"

His arrogance floated around the room in a cloud of haze much like the pot haze in her college apartment when her friends came over to have a good time. She hadn't inhaled then, but she would now. He had a right to be arrogant. She didn't fit neatly into any of his bland brown boxes as he'd suggested because she was a 100 percent fraud, much like the politicians running for office.

Make something up. Chloe's voice echoed in Grace's head, reminding her why she'd come. What would be the one reason that would push Mr. Arrogance's buttons? "He doesn't exist."

Stew on that. Grace rose from her chair, walked over to his window, and pointed down to the street below at people walking by. "I've met my share of men. Some were nice, cordial, and some even made me feel special, but I want more than that. I want something that I haven't found on my own. Something that I've searched long and hard for." She glanced at him to find he'd risen from his seat. "The kind of man I want simply doesn't exist."

"What was missing?" he asked, crossing his arms over his chest as he moved to stand beside her.

"The pitter-patter of my heart when he enters the room. Butterflies doing somersaults in my stomach. The heat from his gaze. The longing for his touch. I crave desire, love, and honesty."

Even now her body trembled just saying the words out loud as though it was therapeutic. Heat scoured her cheeks. One look at her and he'd believe her words. She'd meant them. "Do you have anyone in your databank that would fit my needs?"

****

She was good. He'd give her that. But he knew her game. It was a challenge. Giving him a list of qualities that he'd never be able to fill. What she didn't know about was the private investigation that went into each applicant. He was aware that she was beautiful and smart and her best friend was his competition. Heck, he even knew how she liked her coffee. What she was asking for was chemistry and not something he could find in one of his client's profiles. Time to make her squirm. Turnabout was fair play, after all.

"Do you have anything against sex?"

She turned to look at him and smiled. "I like sex just finc."

"If we take you as a client, you'll be asked to abstain on your dates for the time being."

"That shouldn't be a problem." She turned and crossed her arms beneath her breasts, pushing them up in the little sheer camisole she was wearing. That was a classic move, much like the way she'd seductively crossed her legs. He kept his gaze on hers, ignoring the baser need to check her rack. "I don't need a man's touch to find release."

She'd said the comment with barely a blush. What he wouldn't do to see exactly what it would take to make her turn the color of a rip tomato.

"What about bondage? Anything we should know? There's no sense on pairing you with a vanilla lover if you're more the experimental type. We like to nail our matches right out of the gate. We make them last that way."

Her mouth parted before she quickly snapped it shut and licked her lips. The idea intrigued her. He could read it in her eyes.

"I'd like to think I'm pretty adventurous in bed. I'll try anything once."

Damn her. He'd expected her to gawk and get flustered. Yet she held his gaze, challenging him to produce someone who would fit the bill.

"Tall, dark hair, successful. Secure enough within himself to date an attractive, successful woman. Good in bed, passionate, romantic, muscular body, and smart. He'd have to be able to keep up with you. Does that about describe the type of guy you're looking for?"

"You left out adventurous and open-minded. He'd have to be able to put up with my career choice."

He moistened his lips as he took in the desire shining in her eyes. That was exactly what she wanted. No wonder no man had given her what she needed. They'd never taken the time to read her eyes. They told him everything without her even opening her red kissable lips.

"And if I find you a guy who fits every one of those aspects, you'll agree to the three-date clause in your contract?"

"Are you saying you can find me someone?"

"I'm saying I'll try my best but only after I really get to know you, can I know what type of guy is going to make you tick."

"I thought we just went over that."

"We did. But I need the big picture of how you are around men that are interested in you. Your body language, the attitude you give off, everything if I'm going to find *Mr. Right* and not just *Mr. Right now.*" He sat back down in his chair, pulled out her file, and flipped it open. "We need a week of your time. Can you take time off?"

"A full week?"

"Yes." He signed his name on the contract, turned it to face her, and held out his pen. "An entire week should give us more of an idea of who you are and what type of man would make you happy."

Hesitation flickered in her eyes.

"Those are my terms."

She slipped the pen out of his hand and nibbled her bottom lip between her teeth as she signed. Tossing the pen onto his desk, she picked up her purse and headed for the door. "You've got one full week to get me figured out."

"I'll send the limo to pick you up at seven. Pack a bag with a few casual outfits and a nice dress or two."

"Wait." She spun around. "You didn't say anything about leaving town."

"There's no need to worry, Ms. Thornton. You'll be accompanying me, so you'll be completely safe and never in a compromising situation."

"I'm spending the week with you? That doesn't seem very professional. Are you sure you aren't using your dating company for your own hook-ups?" She teased.

"Do I look like a man that needs to use my company to find women? You're asking me to perform the impossible. I have to go out of town, and I'd like to get started with you right away. I have a feeling I've got my work cut out for me. A week with me is small in comparison to the potential prize. Don't you agree?"

If you enjoyed the excerpt. Grace's book is set to release on 1/1/17 and is available for preorder.

Thank you all for reading my stories. I really do appreciate you! I've been playing around with an entirely new series that should be out in 2017, but not before Becca has her own highlander to contend with and boy is he something else.

Text KATE to 313131 and get a text message on release dates!

Sign up for her newsletters at www.kateallenton.com

Other Books by Kate Allenton

Suggested Reading Order

BENNETT SISTERS BOX SET (Books 1-4 in one bundle, 1218 pages)
BENNETT SISTERS BOX SET VOLUME 2 (Books 5-7 in one bundle, 517 pages}
INTUITION (Book 1)
TOUCH OF FATE (Book 2)
MIND PLAY (Book 3)
THE RECKONING (Book 4)
REDEMPTION (Book 5)
CHANCE ENCOUNTERS (Book 6)

DESTINED HEARTS (Book 7)

PHANTOM PROTECTORS BOX SET (Books 1-4 in one bundle, 964 pages)
RECKLESS ABANDON (Book 1)
BETRAYAL (Book 2)
UNTAMED (Book 3)
GUIDED LOYALTY (Book 4)

CARRINGTON-HILL INVESTIGATIONS
DECEPTION (Book 1)
DEADLY DESIRE (Book 2)

SHIFTER PARADISE BOX SET
NOT MY SHIFTER/ SINFULLY CURSED

KARMA

SOPHIE MASTERSON SERIES/ DIXON SECURITY
LIFTING THE VEIL (Book 1)
BEYOND THE VEIL (Book 2)
VEILED INTENTIONS (Book 3)
VEILED THREATS (Book 4)

THE LOVE FAMILY SERIES
SKYLAR (BOOK1)
DECLAN (BOOK 2)
FLYNN (BOOK 3)
REED (BOOK 4)
LANDON (BOOK 5)
ALEXIS (BOOK 6)
GABE (BOOK 7)

ABOUT THE AUTHOR

Kate has lived in Florida for most of her entire life. She enjoys a quiet life with her husband and two kids.

Kate has pulled all-nighters finishing her favorite books and also writing them. She says she'll sleep when she's dead or when her muse stops singing off key.

She loves creating worlds full of suspense, secrets, hunky men, kick ass heroines, steamy sex and oh yeah the love of a lifetime. Not to mention an occasional ghost and other supernatural talents thrown into the mix.

www.ingramcontent.com/pod-product-compliance
Lightning Source LLC
Chambersburg PA
CBHW072228190626
46809CB00017B/1521
9781944237356